Impossible?

❧

A third boy, behind her, tapped her on the shoulder and whispered, "If you aren't quiet, *He* will find us."

She turned, ready to ask who *He* was. But the boy, dressed in green tights and a green shirt and a rather silly green hat, and smelling like fresh lavender, held a finger up to his lips. They were perfect lips. Like a movie star's. Darla knew him at once.

"Peter," she whispered. "Peter Pan."

He swept the hat off and gave her a deep bow. "Wendy," he countered.

"Well, Darla, actually," she said.

Peter looked at her, and there was nothing nice or laughing or young about his eyes. They were dark and cold and very very old.

Darla shivered.

"*Here* you're a Wendy," he said.

Other Books by Jane Yolen

Twelve Impossible Things Before Breakfast

STORIES BY
JANE YOLEN

MAGIC CARPET BOOKS
HARCOURT, INC.
San Diego   New York   London

First Magic Carpet Books edition 2001
First published 1997
Magic Carpet Books is a trademark of Harcourt, Inc., registered in the United States of America and/or other jurisdictions.

"Curiouser and Curiouser" copyright © 1997 by Jane Yolen; first publication. "Tough Alice" copyright © 1997 by Jane Yolen; first publication. "Mama Gone" copyright © 1991 by Jane Yolen; originally published in *Vampires* (HarperCollins), edited by Jane Yolen and Martin H. Greenberg. "Harlyn's Fairy" copyright © 1993 by Jane Yolen; originally published in *A Wizard's Dozen* (Jane Yolen Books/Harcourt), edited by Michael Stearns. "Phoenix Farm" copyright © 1996 by Jane Yolen; originally published in *Bruce Coville's Book of Magic* (Apple/Scholastic), edited by Bruce Coville. "Sea Dragon of Fife" copyright © 1996 by Jane Yolen; originally published in *Bruce Coville's Book of Monsters II* (Apple/Scholastic), edited by Bruce Coville. "Wilding" copyright © 1995 by Jane Yolen; originally published in *A Starfarer's Dozen* (Jane Yolen Books/Harcourt), edited by Michael Stearns. "The Baby-Sitter" copyright © 1989 by Jane Yolen; originally published in *Things That Go Bump in the Night* (HarperCollins), edited by Jane Yolen and Martin H. Greenberg. "Bolundeers" copyright © 1996 by Jane Yolen; originally published in *A Nightmare's Dozen* (Jane Yolen Books/Harcourt), edited by Michael Stearns. "The Bridge's Complaint" copyright © 1997 by Jane Yolen; first publication. "Brandon and the Aliens" copyright © 1996 by Jane Yolen; originally published in *Bruce Coville's Book of Aliens II* (Apple/Scholastic), edited by Bruce Coville. "Winter's King" copyright © 1992 by Jane Yolen, originally published in *After the King: Stories in Honor of J. R. R. Tolkien* (Tor), edited by Martin H. Greenberg. "Lost Girls" copyright © 1997 by Jane Yolen; first publication. "Running in Place" copyright © 1997 by Jane Yolen; first publication.

The Library of Congress has cataloged the hardcover edition as follows:
Yolen, Jane
Twelve impossible things before breakfast: stories/by Jane Yolen.
p. cm.
Contents: Tough Alice—Mama gone—Harlyn's fairy—Phoenix farm—Sea dragon of Fife—Wilding—The baby-sitter—Bolundeers—The bridge's complaint—Brandon and the aliens—Winter's king—Lost girls.
1. Children's stories, American. [1. Short stories.] I. Title.
PZ7.Y78Tw 1997
[Fic]—dc21   97-667
ISBN 0-15-201524-8
ISBN 0-15-216444-8 pb

Text set in Joanna
Designed by Judythe Sieck

C E G H F D B

Printed in the United States of America

To my fellow traveler in Wonderland,
my wonderful husband, David Stemple

Contents

Curiouser and Curiouser

Why short stories?

I love the compression of the short story. It is as if I can hold the entire thing—theme, plot, character—in the palm of my hand. Novels are messy, untidy propositions. Bits and pieces always seem to get away from both the writer and the reader, no matter how careful we are. But short stories have a containment that nevertheless suggests infinity. A good short story throws long shadows. Like Coyote, the Native American trickster god, the short story throws a shadow that is not black and white but full of color.

This book is a collection of twelve of my fantasy stories for young readers that have never been collected under one roof, so to speak. Three of the stories are absolutely brand-new—so new, in fact, that the price tags are still on them and they are in their original wrapping.

That's a metaphor, of course. But so is this entire collection, I suspect.

Fantasy stories are like that: You say, "This takes place in nineteenth-century Scotland" or "Appalachia in the 1930s" or "Hatfield, Massachusetts, in the seventies," or "Wonderland." You fill the tale with creatures or people that never existed, or you take a spin on stories that are well known and loved. And all the while you talk about the fantastic, you are actually writing about the real world and real emotions, the right-here and the right-now. It is a kind of literary displacement, a way of looking at what worries both writer and reader by glancing out of the corner of one's eye.

Someone once called unicorns "animals that never were and always are." And that's what fantasy is, too.

I titled this volume *Twelve Impossible Things Before Breakfast* after something the White Queen says in *Through the Looking-Glass:*

> "I can't believe that!" said Alice.
>
> "Can't you?" the Queen said in a pitying tone. "Try again: Draw a long breath, and shut your eyes."
>
> Alice laughed. "There's no use trying," she said: "one can't believe impossible things."
>
> "I daresay you haven't had much practice," said the Queen. "When I was your age, I always did it for half-an-hour a day. Why, sometimes I've believed as many as six impossible things before breakfast..."

The reading of fantasy and the writing of it take that kind of practice, too. It all comes easier the younger one is. As a child I had imaginary playmates, spoke to my dolls and heard them answer, played Knights of the Round Table on a pile of rocks in New York's Central Park. I could easily believe six impossible things before breakfast. But somewhere around seventh grade, the one imaginary game I still played—with a friend from ballet school, in which we pretended we were members of the New York City Ballet company, she the prima ballerina and I the choreographer—was played in secret. I was down to one impossible thing, not before breakfast but after school and on Saturdays only.

That secret sharing and the books of fantasy and fairy tales I read were all that was left of my White Queening. But I would not give it up entirely. The worlds of the fantastic, with their mind-stretching, metaphoric, shadow-throwing ways, were still incredibly important to me. I got to learn more about myself and my world by that kind of role playing.

And by reading.

When I grew up to be a writer, I found that my favorite things to write were short fantasies. Impossible things.

And I do my best writing—no surprise here— before breakfast!

Of course, six stories wouldn't have been enough for a book, so it became twelve. Part of the fun of putting this collection together was getting to reread Lewis Carroll. He said an awful lot of wonderful things in those books about writing without actually meaning to. (Or maybe he did!)

"Tut, tut, child!" said the Duchess. "Everything's got a moral, if only you can find it."

and

"Don't grunt," said Alice; "that's not at all a proper way of expressing yourself."

and

"Take care of the sense and the sounds will take care of themselves."

and

"It's ridiculous to leave all the conversation to the pudding!"

and

"The question is," said Alice, "whether you can make words mean so many different things."
"The question is," said Humpty Dumpty, "which is to be master—that's all."

I have tried to be the master in these stories. I am sure they have morals somewhere. I took good care of the sense.

The rest is up to the readers—you, dear puddings.

Jane Yolen

Tough Alice

THE PIG FELL DOWN the rabbit-hole, turning snout over tail and squealing as it went. By the third level it had begun to change. Wonderland was like that, one minute pig, the next pork loin.

It passed Alice on the fourth level, for contrary to the law of physics, she was falling much more slowly than the pig. Being quite hungry, she reached out for it. But no sooner had she set her teeth into its well-done flesh than it changed back into a live pig. Its squeals startled her and she dropped it, which made her use a word her mother had never even heard, much less understood. Wonderland's denizens had done much for Alice's education, not all of it good.

"I promise I'll be a vegetarian if only I land safely," Alice said, crossing her fingers as she fell. At that very moment she hit bottom, landing awkwardly on top of the pig.

"Od-say off-ay!" the pig swore, swatting at her with his hard trotter. Luckily he missed and ran right off toward a copse of trees, calling for his mum.

"The same to you," Alice shouted after him. She didn't know what he'd said but guessed it was in Pig Latin. "You shouldn't complain, you know. After all, you're still whole!" Then she added softly, "And I can't complain, either. If you'd been a pork loin, I wouldn't have had such a soft landing." She had found over the years of regular visits that it was always best to praise Wonderland aloud for its bounty, however bizarre that bounty might be. You didn't want to have Wonderland mad at you. There were things like...the Jabberwock, for instance.

The very moment she thought the word, she heard the beast roar behind her. That was another problem with Wonderland. Think about something, and it appeared. Or *don't think about something*, Alice reminded herself, *and it still might appear*. The Jabberwock was her own personal Wonderland demon. It always arrived sometime during her visit, and someone— her chosen champion—had to fight it, which often signaled an end to her time there.

"Not so soon," Alice wailed in the general direction of the roar. "I haven't had much of a visit yet!" The Jabberwock sounded close, so Alice sighed and raced after the pig into the woods.

The woods had a filter of green and yellow leaves overhead, as lacy as one of her mother's parasols. It really would have been quite lovely if Alice hadn't been in such a hurry. But it was best not to linger anywhere in Wonderland before the Jabberwock was dispatched. Tarrying simply invited disaster.

She passed the Caterpillar's toadstool. It was as big as her uncle Martin, and as tall and pasty white, but it was empty. A sign by the stalk said GONE FISHING. Alice wondered idly if the Caterpillar fished with worms, then shook her head. Worms would be too much like using his own family for bait. Though she had some relatives for whom that might not be a bad idea. Her cousin Albert, for example, who liked to stick frogs down the back of her dress.

Behind her the Jabberwock roared again.

"Bother!" said Alice, and began to zigzag through the trees.

"Haste..." came a voice from above her, "makes wastrels."

Alice stopped and looked up. The Cheshire Cat's grin hung like a demented quarter moon between two limbs of an elm tree.

"Haste," continued the grin, "is a terrible thing to waste."

"That's really not quite right..." Alice began, but the grin went on without pausing:

"Haste is waste control. Haste is wasted on the young. Haste is..."

"You are in a loop," said Alice, and not waiting to hear another roar from the Jabberwock, ran on.

Sunlight pleated down through the trees, wider and wider. Ahead a clearing beckoned. Alice could not help being drawn toward it.

In the center of the clearing a tea party was going on. Hatter to Dormouse to Hare, the conversation was thrown around the long oak table like some erratic ball in a game without rules. The Hatter was saying that teapots made bad pets and the Dormouse that teapots were big pests and the Hare that teapots held big tempests.

Alice knew that if she stopped for tea—chamomile would be nice, with a couple of wholemeal bisquits—the Jabberwock would...

ROAR!

...would be on her in a Wonderland moment. And she hadn't yet found a champion for the fight. So she raced past the tea table, waving her hand.

The tea-party trio did not even stop arguing long enough to call out her name. Alice knew from long experience that Wonderland friends were hardly the kind to send postcards or to remember your birthday, but she had thought they might at least wave back. After all the times she had poured for them, and brought them cakes from the Duchess's pantry! The last trip to Wonderland, she'd even come down the rabbit-hole with her pockets stuffed full of fruit scones because the Dormouse had never tried them with currants. He had spent the entire party after that making jokes about currant affairs, and the Hare had been laughing the whole time. "Hare-sterically," according to the Hatter. *We'd had a simply wonderful time,* Alice thought. It made her a bit cranky that the three ignored her now, but she didn't stop to yell at them or complain. The Jabberwock's roars were too close for that.

Directly across the clearing was a path. On some of her visits the path was there; on others it was twenty feet to the left or right. She raced toward it, hoping the White Knight would be waiting. He was the best of her champions, no matter that he was a bit old and feeble. At least he was always trying. *Quite trying,* she thought suddenly.

She'd even settle for the Tweedle twins, though they fought one another as much as they fought the Jabberwock. Dee and Dum were their names, but— she thought a bit acidly—perhaps Dumb and Dumber more accurately described them.

And then there was the Beamish Boy. She didn't much like him at all, though he *was* the acknowledged Wonderland Ace. Renowned in song and story for beating the Jabberwock, he was too much of a bully for Alice's tastes. And he always insisted on taking the Jabberwock's head off with him. Even for Wonderland, *that* was a messy business.

Of course, this time, with the beast having gotten such an early start, Alice thought miserably, she might need them all. She had hoped for more time before the monster arrived on the scene. Wonderland was usually so much more fun than a vacation at Bath or Baden-Baden, the one being her mother's favorite holiday spot, the other her grandmother's.

But when she got to the path, it was empty. There was no sign of the White Knight or the Tweedles or even the Beamish Boy, who—now that she thought of it—reminded her awfully of Cousin Albert.

And suddenly the Jabberwock's roars were close enough to shake the trees. Green and gold leaves fell around her like rain.

Alice bit her lip. Wonderland might be only a make-believe place, a dreamscape, or a dream escape. But even in a made-up land, there were real dangers. She'd been hurt twice just falling down the rabbit-hole: a twisted ankle one time, a scratched knee another. And once she had pricked her finger on a thorn in the talking flower garden hard enough to draw blood. How the roses had laughed at that!

However, the Jabberwock presented a different kind of danger altogether. He was a horrible creature, nightmarish, with enormous shark-toothed jaws, claws like gaffing hooks, and a tail that could swat her like a fly. There was no doubt in her mind that the Jabberwock could actually kill her if he wished, even in this imaginary land. He had killed off two of her champions on other visits—a Jack of Clubs and the Dodo—and had to be dispatched by the Beamish Boy. She'd never seen either of the champions again.

The thought alone frightened her, and that was when she started to cry.

"No crying allowed," said a harsh, familiar voice.

"No crying aloud," said a quieter voice, but one equally familiar.

Alice looked up. The Red and White Queens were standing in front of her, the White Queen offering a handkerchief that was slightly tattered and not at all clean. "Here, blow!"

Alice took the handkerchief and blew, a sound not unlike the Jabberwock's roar, only softer and infinitely less threatening. "Oh," she said, "thank goodness you are here. You two can save me."

"Not us," said the Red Queen.

"Never us," added the White.

"But then why else have you come?" Alice asked. "I am always saved on this path... wherever this path is at the time."

"The path is past," said the Red Queen. "We are only present, not truly here." As she spoke the dirt path dissolved, first to pebbles, then to grass.

"And you are your own future," added the White Queen.

Alice suddenly found herself standing in the meadow once again, but this time the Hare, the Hatter, and the Dormouse were sitting in stands set atop the table. Next to them were the Caterpillar, his fishing pole over his shoulder; the Cheshire Cat, grinning madly; the White Knight; the Tweedle Twins; the Beamish Boy, in a bright red beanie; the Duchess and her pig baby; and a host of other Wonderlanders. They were exchanging money right and left.

"My money's on you," the White Queen whispered in Alice's ear. "I think you will take the Jabberwock in the first round."

"Take him where?" asked Alice.

"For a fall," the Red Queen answered. Then, shoving a wad of money at the White Queen, she said, "I'll give you three to one against."

"Done," said the White Queen, and they walked off arm-in-arm toward the spectator stands, trailing bits of paper money on the ground.

"But what can I fight the Jabberwock with?" Alice called after them.

"You are a tough child," the White Queen said over her shoulder. "You figure it out."

With that she and the Red Queen climbed onto the table and into the stands, where they sat in the front row and began cheering, the White Queen for Alice, the Red Queen for the beast.

"But I'm not tough at all," Alice wailed. "I've never fought *anything* before. Not even Albert." She had only told on him, and had watched with satisfaction when her mother and his father punished him. Or at least that had seemed satisfactory at first. But when his three older sisters had all persisted in calling "Tattletale twit, your tongue will split" after her for months, it hadn't felt very satisfactory at all.

"I am only," she wept out loud, "a tattletale, not a knight."

"It's not night now!" shouted the Hatter.

"Day! It's day! A frabjous day!" the Hare sang out.

The Beamish Boy giggled and twirled the propeller on the top of his cap.

Puffing five interlocking rings into the air above the crowd, the Caterpillar waved his arms gaily.

And the Jabberwock, with eyes of flame, burst out of the tulgey wood, alternately roaring and burbling. It was a horrendous sound and for a moment Alice could not move at all.

"One, two!" shouted the crowd. "Through and through."

The Jabberwock lifted his tail and slammed it down in rhythm to the chanting. Every time his tail hit the ground, the earth shook. Alice could feel each tremor move up from her feet, through her body, till it seemed as if the top of her head would burst open with the force of the blow. She turned to run.

"She ain't got no vorpal blade," cried the Duchess, waving a fist. "How's she gonna fight without her bloomin' blade?"

At her side, the pig squealed: "Orpal-vay ade-blay."

The Beamish Boy giggled once more.

Right! Alice thought. *I haven't a vorpal blade. Or anything else, for that matter.*

For his part, the Jabberwock seemed delighted that she was weaponless, and he stood up on his hind legs, claws out, to slash a right and then a left in Alice's direction.

All Alice could do was duck and run, duck and run again. The crowd cheered and a great deal more money changed hands. The Red Queen stuffed dollars, pounds, *lira*, and *kroner* under her crown as fast as she could manage. On the other hand, the Dormouse looked into his teapot and wept.

"Oh, Alice," came a cry from the stands, "be tough, child. Be strong." It was the White Queen's voice. "You do not need a blade. You just need courage."

Courage, Alice thought, *would come much easier with a blade.* But she didn't say that aloud. Her tongue felt as if it had been glued by fear to the roof of her mouth. And her feet, by the Queen's call, to the ground.

And still the Jabberwock advanced, but slowly, as if he were not eager to finish her off all at once.

He is playing with me, Alice thought, *rather like my cat, Dinah.* It was not a pleasant thought. She had rescued many a mouse from Dinah's claws and very few of them had lived for more than a minute or two after. She tried to run again but couldn't.

Suddenly she'd quite enough of Wonderland.

But Wonderland was not quite done with Alice.

The Jabberwock advanced. His eyes lit up like skyrockets and his tongue flicked in and out.

"Oh, Mother," Alice whispered. "I am sorry for all the times I was naughty. Really I am." She could scarcely catch her breath, and she promised herself that she would try and die nobly, though she really didn't want to die at all. Because if she died in Wonderland, who would explain it to her family?

The Jabberwock moved closer. He slobbered a bit over his pointed teeth. Then he slipped on a pound note, staggered like Uncle Martin after a party, and his big yellow eyes rolled up in his head. "Ouf," he said.

"Ouf?" Alice whispered. "Ouf?"

It had all been so horrible and frightening, and now, suddenly, it was rather silly. She stared at the Jabberwock and for the first time noticed a little tag on the underside of his left leg. MADE IN BRIGHTON, it said.

Why, he's nothing but an overlarge wind-up toy, she thought. And the very minute she thought that, she began to laugh.

And laugh.

And laugh, until she had to bend over to hold her stomach and tears leaked out of her eyes. She could feel the bubbles of laughter still rising inside, getting up her nose like sparkling soda. She could not stop herself.

"Here, now!" shouted the Beamish Boy, "no laughing! It ain't fair."

The Cheshire Cat lost his own grin. "Fight first, laughter after," he advised. "Or maybe flight first. Or fright first."

The Red Queen sneaked out of the stands and was almost off the table, clutching her crown full of money, when the Dormouse stuck out a foot.

"No going off with that moolah, Queenie," the Dormouse said, taking the crown from her and putting it on top of the teapot.

Still laughing but no longer on the edge of hysteria, Alice looked up at the Jabberwock, who had become frozen in place. Not only was he stiff, but he had turned an odd shade of gray and looked rather like a poorly built garden statue that had been out too long in the wind and rain. She leaned toward him.

"Boo!" she said, grinning.

Little cracks ran across the Jabberwock's face and down the front of his long belly.

"Double boo!" Alice said.

Another crack ran right around the Jabberwock's tail, and it broke off with a sound like a tree branch breaking.

"Triple..." Alice began, but stopped when someone put a hand on her arm. She turned. It was the White Queen.

"You have won, my dear," the White Queen said, placing the Red Queen's crown—minus all the money—on Alice's head. "A true queen is merciful."

Alice nodded, then thought a moment. "But where was the courage in that? All I did was laugh."

"Laughter in the face of certain death? It is the very definition of the Hero," said the White Queen. "The Jabberwock knew it and therefore could no longer move against you. You would have known it yourself much sooner, had that beastly Albert not been such a tattletale."

"But I was the tattletale," Alice said, hardly daring to breathe.

"Who do you think told Albert's sisters?" asked the White Queen. She patted a few errant strands of hair in place and simultaneously tucked several stray dollars back under her crown.

Alice digested this information for a minute, but something about the conversation was still bothering her. Then she had it. "How do you know about Albert?" she asked.

"I'm late!" the White Queen cried suddenly, and dashed off down the road, looking from behind like a large white rabbit.

Alice should have been surprised, but nothing ever really surprised her anymore in Wonderland.

Except...

except...

herself.

Courage, she thought.

Laughter, she thought.

Maybe I'll try them both out on Albert.

And so thinking, she felt herself suddenly rising, first slowly, then faster and faster still, up the rabbit-hole, all the way back home.

Mama Gone

MAMA DIED four nights ago, giving birth to my baby sister, Ann. Bubba cried and cried, "Mama gone," in his little-boy voice, but I never let out a single tear.

There was blood red as any sunset all over the bed from that birthing, and when Papa saw it he rubbed his head against the cabin wall over and over and over and made little animal sounds. Sukey washed Mama down and placed the baby on her breast for a moment. "Remember," she whispered.

"Mama gone," Bubba wailed again.

But I never cried.

By all rights we should have buried her with garlic in her mouth and her hands and feet cut off, what with her being vampire kin and all. But Papa absolutely refused.

"Your Mama couldn't stand garlic," he said when the sounds had stopped rushing out of his mouth and his eyes had cleared. "It made her come all over with rashes. She had the sweetest mouth and hands."

And that was that. Not a one of us could make him change his mind, not even Granddad Stokes or Pop Wilber or any other of the men who come to pay their last respects. And as Papa is a preacher, and a brimstone man, they let it be. The onliest thing he would allow was for us to tie red ribbons 'round her ankles and wrists, a kind of sign like a line of blood. Everybody hoped that would do.

But on the next day she rose from out her grave and commenced to prey upon the good folk of Taunton.

Of course she came to our house first, that being the dearest place she knew. I saw her outside my window, gray as a gravestone, her dark eyes like the holes in a shroud. When she stared in she didn't know me, though I had always been her favorite.

"Mama, be gone," I said, and waved my little cross at her, the one she had given me the very day I'd been born. "Avaunt." The old Bible word sat heavy in my mouth.

She put her hand up on the window frame, and as I watched, the gray fingers turned splotchy pink from all the garlic I had rubbed into the wood.

Black tears dropped from her black eyes, then. But I never cried.

She tried each window in turn, and not a person awake in the house but me. But I had done my work well and the garlic held her out. She even tried the door, but it was no use. By the time she left, I was so sleepy I dropped down right by the door. Papa found me there at cockcrow. He never did ask what I was doing, and if he guessed, he never said.

Little Joshua Greenough was found dead in his crib. The doctor took two days to come over the mountains to pronounce it. By then the garlic around his little bed—to keep him from walking, too—had mixed with death smells. Everybody knew. Even the doctor, and him a city man. It hurt Joshua's mama and papa sore to do the cutting. But it had to be done.

The men came to our house that very noon to talk about what had to be. Papa kept shaking his head all through their talking. But even his being preacher didn't stop them. Once a vampire walks these mountain hollers, there's nary a house or barn that's safe. Nighttime is lost time. And no one can afford to lose much stock.

So they made their sharp sticks out of green wood, the curling shavings littering our cabin floor. Bubba played in them, not understanding. Sukey was busy with the baby, nursing it with a bottle and a sugar teat. It was my job to sweep up the wood curls. They felt slick on one side, bumpy on the other. Like my heart.

Papa said, "I was the one let her turn into a night walker. It's my business to stake her out."

No one argued. Specially not the Greenoughs, their eyes still red from weeping.

"Just take my children," Papa said. "And if

anything goes wrong, cut off my hands and feet and bury me at Mill's Cross, under the stone. There's garlic hanging in the pantry. Mandy Jane will string me some."

So Sukey took the baby and Bubba off to the Greenoughs' house, that seeming the right thing to do, and I stayed the rest of the afternoon with Papa, stringing garlic and pressing more into the windows. But the strand over the door he took down.

"I have to let her in somewhere," he said. "And this is where I'll make my stand." He touched me on the cheek, the first time ever. Papa never has been much for show.

"Now you run along to the Greenoughs', Mandy Jane," he said. "And remember how much your mama loved you. This isn't her, child. Mama's gone. Something else has come to take her place. I should have remembered that the Good Book says, 'The living know that they shall die; but the dead know not anything.' "

I wanted to ask him how the vampire knew to come first to our house, then; but I was silent, for Papa had been asleep and hadn't seen her.

I left without giving him a daughter's kiss, for his mind was well set on the night's doing. But I didn't go down the lane to the Greenoughs' at all. Wearing my triple strand of garlic, with my cross about my neck, I went to the burying ground, to Mama's grave.

It looked so raw against the greening hillside. The

dirt was red clay, but all it looked like to me was blood. There was no cross on it yet, no stone. That would come in a year. Just a humping, a heaping of red dirt over her coffin, the plain pinewood box hastily made.

I lay face down in that dirt, my arms opened wide. "Oh, Mama," I said, "the Good Book says you are not dead but sleepeth. Sleep quietly, Mama, sleep well." And I sang to her the lullaby she had always sung to me and then to Bubba and would have sung to Baby Ann had she lived to hold her.

> Blacks and bays,
> Dapples and grays,
> All the pretty little horses.

And as I sang I remembered Papa thundering at prayer meeting once, "Behold, a pale horse: and his name that sat on him was Death." The rest of the song just stuck in my throat then, so I turned over on the grave and stared up at the setting sun.

It had been a long and wearying day, and I fell asleep right there in the burying ground. Any other time fear might have overcome sleep. But I just closed my eyes and slept.

When I woke, it was dead night. The moon was full and sitting between the horns of two hills. There was a sprinkling of stars overhead. And Mama began to move the ground beneath me, trying to rise.

The garlic strands must have worried her, for she did not come out of the earth all at once. It was the scrabbling of her long nails at my back that woke me. I leaped off that grave and was wide awake.

Standing aside the grave, I watched as first her long gray arms reached out of the earth. Then her head emerged with its hair that was once so gold now gray and streaked with black, and its shroud eyes. And then her body in its winding sheet, stained with dirt and torn from walking to and fro upon the land. Then her bare feet with blackened nails, though alive Mama used to paint those nails, her one vanity and Papa allowed it seeing she was so pretty and otherwise not vain.

She turned toward me as a hummingbird toward a flower, and she raised her face up and it was gray and bony. Her mouth peeled back from her teeth and I saw that they were pointed and her tongue was barbed.

"Mama gone," I whispered in Bubba's voice, but so low I could hardly hear it myself.

She stepped toward me off that grave, lurching down the hump of dirt. But when she got close, the garlic strands and the cross stayed her.

"Mama."

She turned her head back and forth. It was clear she could not see with those black shroud eyes. She only sensed me there, something warm, something alive, something with blood running like satisfying streams through blue veins.

"Mama," I said again. "Try and remember."

That searching awful face turned toward me again, and the pointy teeth were bared once more. Her hands reached out to grab me, then pulled back.

"Remember how Bubba always sucks his thumb with that funny little noise you always said was like a little chuck in its hole. And how Sukey hums through her nose when she's baking bread. And how I listened to your belly to hear the baby. And how Papa always starts each meal with the blessing on things that grow fresh in the field."

The gray face turned for a moment toward the hills, and I wasn't even sure she could hear me. But I had to keep trying.

"And remember when we picked the blueberries and Bubba fell down the hill, tumbling head-end over. And we laughed until we heard him, and he was saying the same six things over and over till long past bed."

The gray face turned back toward me and I thought I saw a bit of light in the eyes. But it was just reflected moonlight.

"And the day Papa came home with the new ewe lamb and we fed her on a sugar teat. You stayed up all the night and I slept in the straw by your side."

It was as if stars were twinkling in those dead

eyes. I couldn't stop staring, but I didn't dare stop talking, either.

"And remember the day the bluebird stunned itself on the kitchen window and you held it in your hands. You warmed it to life, you said. To life, Mama."

Those stars began to run down the gray cheeks.

"There's living, Mama, and there's dead. You've given so much life. Don't be bringing death to these hills now." I could see that the stars were gone from the sky over her head; the moon was setting.

"Papa loved you too much to cut your hands and feet. You gotta return that love, Mama. You gotta."

Veins of red ran along the hills, outlining the rocks. As the sun began to rise, I took off one strand of garlic. Then the second. Then the last. I opened my arms. "Have you come back, Mama, or are you gone?"

The gray woman leaned over and clasped me tight in her arms. Her head bent down toward mine, her mouth on my forehead, my neck, the outline of my little gold cross burning across her lips.

She whispered, "Here and gone, child, here and gone," in a voice like wind in the coppice, like the shaking of willow leaves. I felt her kiss on my cheek, a brand.

Then the sun came between the hills and hit her full in the face, burning her as red as earth. She smiled at me and then there were only dust motes in the air, dancing. When I looked down at my feet, the grave dirt was hardly disturbed but Mama's gold wedding band gleamed atop it.

I knelt down and picked it up, and unhooked the chain holding my cross. I slid the ring onto the chain, and the two nestled together right in the hollow of my throat. I sang:

> Blacks and bays,
> Dapples and grays . . .

and from the earth itself, the final words sang out,

> All the pretty little horses.

That was when I cried, long and loud, a sound I hope never to make again as long as I live.

Then I went back down the hill and home, where Papa still waited by the open door.

Harlyn's Fairy

HARLYN HAD NOT EXPECTED to see a fairy that day in the garden. Buttercups, yes. And the occasional early rose. And varieties of plants with odd names like snow-in-summer and bachelor's button. Aunt Marilyn loved to plant and grow flowers, almost as much as she liked to watch birds. But if she had ever seen a fairy in her garden, she had neglected to tell Harlyn about it.

Yet there it was, flittering about on two fast-beating wings as veined and as transparent as stained glass. It sounded like a slightly dotty insect and was pulling the petals off the only red rose in bloom.

Harlyn drew in a sharp, surprised breath. When she exhaled, the wind nearly blew the fairy halfway across the arbor.

"Whooosh!" the fairy cried out. When it had gotten its tiny wings untangled at last, it flew back toward her, shaking its fist and scolding in a voice that sounded as if it were being run backward at the wrong speed. Harlyn didn't understand a word.

After a half-minute harangue, the fairy flew down to the ground and picked up the dropped petals, stuffing them into a silvery sack. Then it zipped off in the direction of the trees, canting to one side because of the sack's weight.

But how much can rose petals possibly weigh? Harlyn mused.

When the fairy disappeared into the copse of trees, Harlyn turned.

"Oh, Aunt Marilyn," she said aloud, "boy, do you have some explaining to do."

"A *fairy*?" said Aunt Marilyn, shaking her head. "Don't be silly, child. It must have been a ruby-throated hummingbird. They move that way." Her hand described a sort of twittery up-and-down zigzag motion not unlike the fairy's flight pattern.

"A fairy," Harlyn said. "It spoke to me. Well, yelled, actually."

"And what did this *fairy* say?" Clearly Aunt Marilyn did not believe her.

"How should I know?" Harlyn answered. "I don't speak Fairy. But it wasn't happy, that's for sure."

"It was pretty hot out there, dear..." Aunt Marilyn began in her *understanding* voice, the one she'd used since Harlyn's mother's latest breakdown brought Harlyn once again to her house.

Harlyn nodded, though they both knew the day was really on the cool side.

"How about a peanut-butter sandwich?" That was all Aunt Marilyn was going to say about the fairy; of this Harlyn was sure.

Harlyn ate the sandwich and drank a glass of milk while Aunt Marilyn hovered over her, carefully watching for signs of something like the delusions Harlyn's mother had entertained on and off ever since she had been a teenager. Harlyn was well aware of this scrutiny; she even welcomed it, usually.

"It *was* hot out, Aunt Marilyn, hotter than at home. And there were *lots* of birds," Harlyn said at last.

"Nothing else?" This was Aunt Marilyn's way of offering a truce without actually saying the dreaded f-word, *fairy*.

"Nothing else," Harlyn answered.

"I have to go shopping, and you can come with me if you want to..." Aunt Marilyn clearly wanted to shop alone, and Harlyn was really too old to need a baby-sitter, having already done a bit of sitting for other kids herself.

"I'd rather stay home," she said. "I brought a book." She had *The Hobbit*, which she was about to read for the fourth time.

Aunt Marilyn sighed and picked up her pocket-book and binoculars. "I won't be long."

She will, though, Harlyn thought, *especially if an interesting bird suddenly crosses her path.*

As soon as the car left the driveway, Harlyn bolted out the back door and into the garden. This time the fairy was harvesting handfuls of mint from the herb patch. The little silvery pack was almost full.

Turning her face carefully to one side so as not to breathe on the fairy, Harlyn watched it out of the corner of her eye. Clearly it knew she was there, for she was much too big to be ignored. It ignored her nonetheless.

"Can I help?" she whispered.

The answer was as indistinguishable as before, high pitched and foreign and fast, but Harlyn took it as a *yes.* She knelt down and began to pull bits of mint leaves off, tearing them into tiny pieces that she handed to the fairy. The fairy took them, not at all gratefully, and tore them into even smaller bits, then stuffed them into the pack until it was overflowing. Then, without so much as a wave, it flew off.

"Well—and thanks to you, too!" Harlyn called after it.

She said nothing about seeing the fairy again when Aunt Marilyn came home. And what with one thing and another—making Toll House cookies and peanut-butter pie and helping Aunt Marilyn put stamps in her albums—the day flew past. At bedtime Harlyn borrowed a bunch of bird books, knowing that—though they had wings—fairies were certainly not birds. Probably not even a related genus or species. But the books were worth checking out anyway.

Besides, it pleased Aunt Marilyn, who didn't like Harlyn reading books like *The Hobbit*. She thought fantasy stories were trashy, even dangerous, and said so often. "Empty make-believe" was one of her favorite phrases.

Harlyn checked through the section on hummingbirds with special care. They were certainly the right size, and their wings beat as quickly as fairies' might. So it was just possible that...

"Nuts!" Harlyn said aloud. "It *was* a fairy. It spoke to me and it was carrying a bag." Besides, her mother's delusions were about people trying to kill her and UFO aliens kidnapping her. Crazy stuff. Harlyn put the book down. She knew what she'd seen.

Harlyn dreamed all night of hummingbirds who called her name, and of eagles the size of roses quarreling with the hummers. When she awoke, the sky was gray and rain was slanting down so hard that the rose arbor looked as if it were behind a very dirty curtain.

"House cleaning," Aunt Marilyn said in a cheery voice. "That's all you can do on a day like this."

Harlyn thought wistfully of her book. She was at

the riddles part, which she loved. But it wouldn't do to make a fuss. That would mean a well-intentioned lecture from Aunt Marilyn with unsubtle references to living in fantasy worlds. So Harlyn helped clean.

It was while she was working on the windows over the kitchen sink, the ones usually kept open for the robin who had adopted Aunt Marilyn, that she found a pink rubber band and three red berries, dried and shriveled, set side-by-side. Harlyn didn't want to climb off the counter just to throw them away, so she shoved them into her pocket, meaning to dump them when she was finished with the windows.

"And what," she said to herself as she scrubbed at one particular spot on the windowpane, "have I got in my pocketses, my precious?" She hissed with gusto, like Gollum, or like an overworked kettle. But by the time she'd finished the windows, she'd forgotten to throw out the berries.

In the afternoon the rain ended and a glorious rainbow settled over the arbor. The lawn was so damp, Harlyn went out barefooted, but she couldn't find the fairy anywhere. Not even a trace of it.

Though what could be considered a trace of a fairy? she wondered. Torn rose petals? There were plenty of those. A second rose, a yellow one on a different bush, had opened, and the wind accompanying the rain had beaten off some of its petals, scattering them like a miser's treasure onto the lawn.

It was just when she had decided there was no

fairy to be found and her imagination had indeed gotten the best of her that Harlyn heard a strange, tiny, thin wail, a meager thread of sound. It was not like anything, or at least not like anything she had heard before. She followed it, rather as if winding it up around her finger, until she came to an old and shaggy birch tree at the edge of the garden, in the untidy "natural" part she liked best, which ran down to a little stream.

The sound was louder now, but not any more robust, and Harlyn cast about for whatever was making that sound. For a moment the sound seemed high, then it was low, then somewhat oddly in between.

And then she saw a line of ants—rather large ants, about the size of her knuckle, the stinging kind, dark and purposeful—marching around the tree's trunk. They had been disguised at first by the birch's dark patches, but soon she could distinguish them against the white. They were heading toward the thicket on the right, where there were mean and wicked-looking thorns. When Harlyn squinched her eyes, she could see that the ants in front were carrying something tiny and light colored. She bent over and stared and, at last, realized that what they were carrying was a teeny-tiny baby—no bigger than her pinkie nail—wrapped in a yellow rose petal. The baby was waving its little arms and crying. It was that crying that Harlyn had heard.

Suddenly the grown-up fairy simply materialized

above the marching ants, dithering at them and swooping and swerving overhead, shaking its tiny fist and screaming. It tried several times to snatch the baby, but the ants fought it off fiercely each time, hardly pausing in their march toward the thicket.

For a moment Harlyn watched, fascinated. They were all so small—ants and fairy and baby—that she could hardly feel anything but amusement at first. But then the fairy saw her and broke off its chittering attack on the ants to fly her way, waving its tiny arms and haranguing her again in its high-speed language. Without thinking, Harlyn put her hand out and the fairy alighted on her thumb.

When Harlyn brought her hand to her eyes, she could see that the fairy was unmistakably female— probably the baby's mother. And she was crying and yelling at the same time.

"All right. All right," Harlyn said. At her voice the fairy was silent. "I'll see what I can do." She waved her hand gently, which sent the fairy sailing back into the air.

Harlyn snapped off a dead branch of the birch and, using it as a kind of a whisk broom, tried to brush the closest ants away. But as if they had some dark magic binding them together, they scattered for a moment and then re-formed their line, marching on and on with the fairy child toward the thicket of prickers and humming an evil-sounding ant chant.

Harlyn tried a second and a third time with her

stick broom, then angrily tried stomping on some of
the ants. But each time she did, the rest of them scattered and returned.

The fairy flew up by her ear and chittered loudly
at her.

"Well, I don't know what *else* to do!" Harlyn
shouted back, loudly enough to make the fairy shove
her tiny hands over her tiny ears. "I mean, it's like
they have magic or something. And I don't. You
know—*magic*! Ugga-bugga-abracadabra-zam-booie!"
She waggled her fingers.

The fairy went "Oh-ah!" in a high-pitched voice
and suddenly fluttered around her three times at a
speed that made Harlyn's eyes cross. And at each
turning, the fairy sprinkled Harlyn with some kind
of powder that must have been mainly ragweed because it made Harlyn sneeze and sneeze and sneeze
until her nose dripped and her eyes filled up.

"Enough already!" Harlyn cried, wiping a hand
across her eyes. When she could see again, everything
around her seemed awfully green.

And awfully big.

But that was wrong. What she meant was, she
seemed suddenly and awfully small. And she hadn't
felt anything, except—well—the sneezing. Of course
she wasn't as small as the fairy, who was still raging
at her and flinging the powder this way and that, but
she was small enough so that the grass was suddenly
like a high fence all about her and the marching ants

in front of her were as large as motorcycles—and looked as dangerous.

"Oh, great, you stupid fairy!" Harlyn shouted. "I might have done some good at my regular size. But what am I going to be able to do when I'm this small?" She grabbed up a nearby stick—it would have been a twig if she were at her regular height—for protection. Then she swung it wildly at the ants. They scattered again, all but the front three. Of course they *would* be the biggest and meanest looking. And they were the ones taking turns carrying the baby.

"Oh, great!" Harlyn said again, for the three were heading purposefully and unrelentingly toward the thicket and she could hear the rest of the ants starting to re-form behind her. Pretty soon she would be in an ant sandwich. It was not a pleasant thought.

And then she remembered...and flung the stick aside.

"What *have* I got in my pocketses, my precious?" The rubber band had gotten proportionally smaller with her, but it still had its stretch. She pulled on it to test its bounce, then reached back into her pocket for the three hard dried berries. Planting her feet firmly, she pulled out one of the berries, dropped it into the rubber-band sling, and let fly toward the three ants carrying the fairy's child, screaming out all the movie war cries she could think of: "Geronimo! Cowabunga! Heigh-ho, Silver, ants, and away..."

She wasn't quite as accurate with the slingshot as she was with spitballs, the berries being both larger and heavier than the rolled-paper wads she was used to. But the berry dropped like a bomb on top of the middle ant's head, startling it so it dropped its hold on the baby and ran off to sulk in the grass. The other two ants, though, grabbed up the little bundle and, as if of one mind, marched on urgently toward the thorns.

Harlyn bit her lip. "OK, you suckers," she whispered, putting the second berry in the sling. She let fly. It caught the left-hand ant on the leg.

The ant dropped its hold on the blanket and began to walk in circles.

Harlyn dived forward, shouting, "Say uncle, you ant!" and laughing at the same time, mostly because she was scared stiff.

The lead ant was now inches from the thicket, and from this close the thorny entrance looked sharp as doom. Harlyn put the last berry in the sling and was about to let it rip when something bit down on her ankle from behind. It stung like stink.

"Ow!" she cried, reaching down. The last berry dropped out of the sling and rolled away. Harlyn kicked back with her injured leg, connecting with the ant's head. Then, hobbling forward, she grabbed up her stick again and jammed it between the lead ant's jaws and the yellow rose-petal blanket. Surprised, the ant opened its mouth and the baby dropped out.

There was a swoosh of wings and the mother fairy slipped down startlingly fast on a quiver of air, grabbed the child before it hit the ground, and winged back up without a by-your-leave. And there was Harlyn, left all alone to face a line of large, angry ants.

What will Aunt Marilyn say? Harlyn wondered briefly. Even more briefly she wondered, *Will Mother think the space aliens got me?* Then she hefted the stick as if it were Robin Hood's staff and prepared for her final fight.

Just as the line of ants closed in, chanting and snuffling and breathing out some kind of dark, thick smell, a fine mist began to fall and Harlyn started sneezing and sneezing, again and again and again.

Blinded by the tears in her eyes, she felt her way backward, somehow eluding the line of ants, until she reached the trunk of a tree. Quickly she crawled around the back. Then she managed to creep into a corner of a crevice between the roots.

She must have fallen asleep, exhausted from the fight or the allergy attack, because she could only faintly hear the fairy shouting at her, "Harlyn... Harlyn..." When she opened her eyes, she realized the voice was really Aunt Marilyn, calling from the door. Harlyn's leg ached and she was unaccountably dirty and...

"There you are," Aunt Marilyn said. "I've been frantic. I couldn't find you anywhere, and then there was this enormous infestation of horrible gigantic ants that seemed absolutely immune to my spray, and..." She paused and ran a hand through her thick gray hair. "And now, sweetie, a call from the hospital saying your mom won't be released anytime soon."

"Not coming home," Harlyn whispered. She was surprised she did not feel worse.

"And look at your leg! That's some bite. Did those ants get you? We need to put something on it at once. Their bites can trigger allergic reactions, you know."

Aunt Marilyn took Harlyn inside and soaked the bite in peroxide, which hurt, but not exactly, and then put antibiotic cream on it, which felt good, but not exactly.

"I could just kill those ants, sweetie," Aunt Marilyn said.

"I know you could," Harlyn said. She gave Aunt Marilyn a hug; then, as there was still some time before dinner, she went back out into the garden.

By the tree was a twig, and twined around its top in a complicated knot was the rubber band. At the base of the twig were red rose petals. The whole thing looked very much like some sort of memorial. A line of very large ants were carefully avoiding the site. Of the fairies—mother and child—there was no other sign.

"Empty make-believe?" Harlyn whispered aloud. "Space aliens?" Then she shook her head. She knew better. But she wouldn't tell her mother or Aunt Marilyn. Especially Aunt Marilyn. After all, Harlyn expected she would be living here for a good long time, and it would be better to protect her aunt from anything as real as a fairy.

Phoenix Farm

E MOVED INTO GRANDMA'S farm right after our apartment house burned down along with most of the neighborhood. Even without the fire, it had not been a good California summer, dry as popcorn and twice as salty, what with all the sweat running down our faces.

I didn't mind so much—the fire, I mean. I had hated that apartment, with its pockmarked walls and the gang names scribbled on the stoop. Under my bedroom window someone had painted the words "Someday, sugar, you gonna find no one in this world gonna give you sweet." The grammar bothered me more than what it said.

Mama cried, though. About the photos, mostly. And about all her shoes having burned up. She has real tiny feet and her one vanity is shoes. She can buy the model stuff for really cheap. But it's not just the photos and the shoes. She cries about everything these days. It's been that way since Daddy died.

Ran off. That's what Nicky says. A week before the fire. *Couldn't take it. The recession and all. No job. No hope.*

Mama says it won't be forever, but I say he died. I can deal with it that way.

And besides, we don't want him back.

So we got ready to head for Grandma's farm up in the valley, with only the clothes we'd been wearing; our cat, Tambourine; and Mama's track medals, all fused together. She found them when the firefighters let us go back upstairs to sort through things. Nicky grabbed a souvenir, too. His old basketball. It was flat and blackened, like a pancake someone left on the stove too long.

I looked around and there was nothing I wanted to take. Nothing. All that I cared about had made it through the fire: Mama, Nicky, and Tam. It was as if we could start afresh and all the rest of it had been burned away. But as we were going down the stairs—the iron stairs, not the wooden ones inside, which were all gone—I saw the most surprising thing. On the thirteenth step up from the bottom, tucked against the riser, was a nest. It was unburnt, unmarked, the straw that held it the rubbed-off gold of a wheat field. A piece of red string ran through it, almost as if it had been woven on a loom. In the nest was a single egg.

It didn't look like any egg I'd ever seen before, not dull white or tan like the eggs from the store. Not even a light blue like the robin's egg I'd found the one summer we'd spent with Grandma at the farm. This was a shiny, shimmery gray-green egg with a red vein—the red thread—cutting it in half.

"Look!" I called out. But Mama and Nicky were already in the car, waiting. So without thinking it all the way through—like, what was I going to do with an egg, and what about the egg's mother, and what if it broke in the car or, worse, hatched—I picked it up and stuck it in the pocket of my jacket. Then, on second thought, I took off the jacket and made a kind of nest of it, and carefully carried the egg and my jacket down the rest of the stairs.

When I got into the car, it was the very first time I had ever ridden in the back all alone without complaining. And all the way to the farm, I kept the jacket-nest and its egg in my lap. All the way.

Grandma welcomed us, saying, "I'm not surprised. Didn't I tell you?" Meaning that Daddy wasn't with us. She and Mama didn't fight over it, which was a surprise on its own. Neighbors of Grandma's had collected clothes for us. It made us feel like refugees, which is an awkward feeling that makes you prickly and cranky most of the time. At least that's how I felt until I found a green sweater that exactly matches my eyes and Nicky found a Grateful Dead T-shirt. There were no shoes Mama's size. And no jobs nearby, either.

I stashed the egg in its jacket-nest on the dresser

Mama and I shared. Nicky, being the only boy, got his own room. Mama never said a word about the egg. It was like she didn't even see it. I worried what she'd say if it began to smell.

But the days went by and the egg never did begin to stink. We got settled into our new school. I only thought about Daddy every other day. And I found a best friend right away. Nicky had girls calling him after dinner for the first time. So we were OK.

Mama wasn't happy, though. She and Grandma didn't exactly quarrel, but they didn't exactly get along, either. Being thankful to someone doesn't make you like them. And since Mama couldn't find a job, they were together all day long.

Then one evening my new best friend, Ann Marie, was over. We were doing homework together up in my room. It was one of those coolish evenings and the windows were closed, but it was still pretty bright outside, considering.

Ann Marie suddenly said, "Look! Your egg is cracking open."

I looked up and she was right. We hadn't noticed anything before, because the crack had run along the red line. When I put my finger on the crack, it seemed to pulse.

"Feel that!" I said.

Ann Marie touched it, then jerked back as if she had been burned. "I'm going home now," she said.

"But, Ann Marie, aren't you the one who dragged me to see all those horror movies and—"

"Movies aren't real," she said. She grabbed up her books and ran from the room.

I didn't even say good-bye. The egg had all my attention, for the gray-green shell seemed to be taking little breaths, pulsing in and out, in and out, like a tiny brittle ocean. Then the crack widened, and as if there were a lamp inside, light poured out.

Nicky came in then, looking for some change on the dresser.

"Neat!" he said when he saw the light. "Do you know what kind of bird it's going to be? Did you look it up in Dad—" And then he stopped, because all of Daddy's books had been burned up. Besides, we didn't mention him anymore. And since we hadn't heard from him at all, it was like he really *was* dead.

"No," I said. "And I don't think it's any ordinary bird that you would find in an ordinary book."

"A lizard, you think?"

Never taking my eyes off the egg, I shook my head. How stupid could he be? With that light coming out? A dragon, maybe. Then the phone rang downstairs and he ran out of the room, expecting, I guess, that it would be Courtney or Brittany or another of his girlfriends named after spaniels. Talking to them was more important to him than my egg.

But I continued to watch. I was the only one

watching when it hatched. How such a large bird got into such a small egg, I'll never know. But that's magic for you. It rose slowly out of the egg, pushing the top part of the shell with its golden head. Its beak was golden, too, and curved like one of those Arabian swords. Its eyes were hooded and dark, without a center. When it stared at me, I felt drawn in.

The bird gave a sudden kind of shudder and humped itself farther out of the egg, and its wings were blue and scarlet and gold, all shimmery, like some seashells when they're wet. It shook out its wings, and they were wide enough to touch from one side of the dresser to the other, the individual feathers throwing off sparkles of light.

Another shudder, and the bird stood free of the egg entirely, though a piece of shell still clung to the tip of one wing. I reached over and freed it, and it seared my fingers—the touch of the feather, not the shell. The bird's scarlet body and scaly golden feet pulsed with some kind of heat.

"What *are* you?" I whispered, then stuck my burnt fingers in my mouth to soothe them.

If the bird could answer me, it didn't; it just pumped its wings, which seemed to grow wider with each beat. The wind from them was a Santa Ana, hot and heavy and thick.

I ran to the window and flung it wide, holding the curtain aside.

The bird didn't seem to notice my effort, but still

it flew unerringly outside. I saw it land once on a fencepost; a second time, on the roof of Grandma's barn. Then it headed straight toward the city, the setting sun making a fire in its feathers.

When I couldn't see it anymore, I turned around. The room smelled odd—like the ashes of a fire, but like something else, too. Cinnamon, maybe. Or cloves.

I heard the doorbell. It rang once, then a second time. Grandma and Mama were off visiting a neighbor. Nicky was still on the phone. I ran down the stairs and flung the door wide open.

Daddy was standing there, a new beard on his face and a great big Madame Alexander doll in his arms.

"I got a job, baby. In Phoenix. And a house rented. With a real backyard. I didn't know about the fire, I didn't know where you all had gone. My letters came back and the phone didn't connect and..."

"Daddy!" I shouted, and he dropped the box to scoop me up against his chest. As I snuggled my face against his neck, I smelled that same smell: ashes and cinnamon, maybe cloves. Where my burnt fingers tangled in his hair they hurt horribly.

Grandma would be furious. Nicky and Mama might be, too. But I didn't care. There's dead. And there's not.

Sometimes it's better to rise up out of the ashes, singing.

Sea Dragon
of Fife

WE FOUND the monster near McBridey's well on Sunday, after the long kirk service in which Reverend Dougal preached against the dangers of the sea. He preaches that one at least twice a year, and most parishioners never tire of it.

The monster wasn't much, as monsters go. A couple of horns, a snubbed snout, nine stubby talons—one was missing, probably torn off in a fight—and a tail with three barbs, all quite worn. But as it was the only monster discovered in Fife this spring, we had to track him.

He died early Monday morning, not from his wounds but from the lack of a blood meal. We had tracked him to his lair by the trail of ichor, but we did not dare go in. We just waited him out, knowing that a hungry monster goes quite quickly. One minute snarling and swearing in his monster tongue, and the next minute dead. It's never pretty, but it's lucky for us; otherwise we'd be overrun with monsters. When we heard the thud in his cave, we waited another hour just to be sure. Then McBridey himself crawled in and stuck a good stout Anster hook in the beast. We towed him out to sea, trawling for a certain sea dragon.

It was Angus McLeod's wife, Annie, who baited the lines for us, sitting on the stone stairs in front of their house and smoking her clay pipe. A braw woman, that, not a bit afraid of any land monster, though even dead it was quite a fright. Most of the women in the cities would have run screaming from it. But Annie was a fisherman's wife and had seen a lot in her life. Besides, she'd just that spring lost her two oldest sons to a great sea dragon, one of the ferocious deep-sea meat-eaters. They'd been plucked off their father's Zulu in front of his disbelieving eyes. Annie was not about to lose Robert, her twelve-year-old, who was next off to sea. She wanted that dragon caught and cooked. So she baited the hook with as much ease as she baited the sma' lines with mussels for her husband's boat. Not a blink out of her, not over the monster's horns or snout or talons or barbed tail. All the while the smoke from her pipe curled about her head like a halo.

"Done," Annie said, standing and stretching. Like all the McLeods, she was never one for excess conversation.

We loaded the bait monster into McLeod's own
Zulu and the little boat wallowed a bit under the
weight, but it was no heavier than a load of haddock,
I suppose. And then we were off, the red sails floating
nicely on a flanny wind, with its soft and unexpected
breezes. Annie waved to us from shore, her other
hand tight on young Robert. He was pulling away
from her a bit. Twelve is big enough for a man, but
she was not about to let him go till that dragon was
dead.

It was a mackerel sky, so we didn't need much
sail. Still, a Zulu's red sail can look like a banner, and
so we flew it to signal that dragon we were coming.
It looked a bit like the old clan banners the Highland
men hoisted when they went off to fight at Sterling
and at Bannockburn. Lord, we were sure of ourselves.
Besides, we'd our guns with us, and a couple of har-
poons as well. And a barrel of gunpowder. We would
not be snatched up, like McLeod's two boys, without
a fight.

But we had to come home early, the bait taken—
snubbed snout, nine talons, and all. And not so much
as a dragon's claw to show for it. McLeod was in a
foul mood, for the dragon had taken not only the
bait but a bit of his red sail as well. He was as
"thrawn as a wulf," so his wife said when we landed,
meaning he was contrary and angry and not to be
fooled with. He snapped at her and she threw a bit
of netting at him. So he took himself off to the pub

and did not come home until the wee hours of the morning.

Annie knew better than to wait up for him. But she should have stayed awake on account of Robert. That boy had been growing in leg and thigh and heart since his brothers' deaths, and he would not be treated like a bairn, a child, anymore. He had made up his mind. He was stubborn, like all the McLeods.

When the old man came home from the pub past midnight, his Zulu was gone. And gone, too, was young Robert.

Annie was weeping on the shore in the moonlight, crying, "Robert, Robert..." and even occasionally "Robin..." which was the bairn's name she had had for him. Her skirt was kilted up and soaking wet, for she had been in the sea after him. But he had never looked back, not even to wave. He did not dare. He was afraid if he saw his mam crying and calling for him, it would unman him, or so he said later.

He had gone without bait, except for his own self, and with no help at the oars but the good Lord above. He'd gone to get that brother-killing dragon or die.

McLeod tried to bring Annie inside but she continued to weep on the shore till all of Anster was awake. And then didn't all the women weep with her, for there was not a one of them in Anster who didn't count the boy gone for good.

"If he is lucky," McAllister said, "he'll be

drowned first." He didn't say "and eaten after," but we were surely all thinking it.

At first light we went out in three swift Fifies to look for him, but no trace of boy or boat did we find. So we had to return home to mourn him like his brothers, with McLeod and his Annie weeping in one another's arms on the pier. A weeping man is a sore sight indeed. But we were too soon with our burial, though we didn't know it then. And what we would hear from Robert after was a story indeed.

Robert had sailed north and then west till the wind dropped like a gannet into the water. He just sat there in the Zulu, becalmed, with nothing to do except to think. He was remembering his older brothers, Jamie and Matthew, who had been his idols, the two of them as alike as twins though a year or more apart. They both had had sweethearts in Anster, fisher lassies who had not taken their loss with any ease, but still came to the cottage and sat with his mam and talked of Jamie and Matthew as if the boys were somehow still alive.

It did not occur to Robert as he sat in the dark on the ocean that he, too, would most likely die there in the dragon's great maw. Lads that age have no fear in them, even fisher lads who have the sea in their bones. He rowed a bit, then rested, then rowed a bit more.

When the sun came up, he was far from sight of

land. The sky was first red, then blue, above him, the water black below. Robert had been out on the water from the time he had been a babe in arms, but never this far out on his own. Still, he trusted his own skills and his father's little Zulu, it being sturdy and competent like himself. The sun had warmed him by then, so he took off his oilskin. His jersey was coat enough. And it was that small thing that saved him. The Lord's ways, as Reverend Dougal likes to say, are as unfathomable as the deepest part of the sea.

No sooner had Robert shrugged off his coat and set it on a hook on the mast then a snaky green head and neck, as tall as the mast itself, lifted out of the sea and ripped the oilskin from its resting place. Used to men in their coats being a soft prey, the dragon had mistaken skin for man. Its great hinged jaws, fringed with rows of teeth, opened and closed on the slick coat and carried it triumphantly back into the sea.

Now, Robert was a quick lad—though no quicker than Matthew or Jamie, just luckier. As soon as he had gotten over his startle, he grabbed up the threaded gaffing hook and leaped over the side of the boat after the beast. Though he had never been a horse rider, knowing only the white mares of the sea—those great waves that break on the East Neuk shore—he landed astride the sea dragon's neck and knew enough to hold tight with his thighs and grab 'round with his arms. The sea dragon's scales were as cold and as slippery with foam as a fish's, and the edges of each scale sharp as a honed knife. In the sun the dragon glowed with iridescence, like a hundred sharpened rainbows under him.

Robert had but a moment to be frightened at what he had just done. And a moment to realize that his legs and palms were being slivered. Then he remembered his brothers, whose bodies had never been found.

"You great lump of putrescence!" he cried. "You murthering, heathenish fish!" It was a long speech for a McLeod. Paying no attention to his own wounds, he reared back, holding on to the neck with his legs and one hand, and set the hook with all his might into the monster's glistening eye.

The pain of that must have been something horrendous, for the dragon screamed, a sound so loud it was heard all the way to Arbroath, where the fishermen mistook it for a foghorn though the day was fully clear of the haar, the sea mist.

The dragon tossed its head back and forth, its scales now aglitter with green blood as well as foam. Robert was flung off on the third toss, but luck held him again in its fist, and he landed against the Zulu's bow. Climbing back into the boat, he realized he still had the rope end of the hook in his hand. This he made fast three times around the mast, then he tied it with his father's best knot. Then he sank down, exhausted and bleeding from a hundred small cuts.

But there was no time to rest or to tend his wounds for, in its agony, the sea dragon had headed down to its watery lair. And if it had gone all the way, that would have been the end—of Zulu and Robert, both. But the hook—luck three times—had caught up under the monster's eyebone, and the pain when the rope had pulled tight was so great that the dragon gave up its dive and turned back to the water's surface, where it fell onto the flat of the sea. There it began to swim, paddling awkwardly—for it was a deep-sea creature—into the east end of the firth, tail and flippers lashing the water into a froth that bubbled onto the beaches as far west as Queensferry, and upsetting a bevy of pleasure boats out for the day.

Of course it dragged the little Zulu behind, with the exhausted Robert hanging on to the gunnels in terror. But there was nothing he could do except pray.

The morning and afternoon sped by and night was coming on, and the dragon kept swimming westward, towing the boat and Robert in its wake.

They passed the Isle of May after dark, startling puffins off their nests, then circled three times around Bass Rock, and all the while that dragon tried to rid itself of its unwanted cargo. Then it headed back east again and out to the open sea.

That hook, made of cold iron, held fast in the fey creature's head. The Zulu, being of good East Neuk make, did not break up. And Robert, like a true Scot, went from terror to anger to cool courage. His wounds stopped bleeding and scabbed over; his heart scabbed over, too. He became a man on that first night, and something even greater by dawn.

He was to say, later, that there had been porpoises on either side of his boat, encouraging him, some riding ahead like beacons and some skirling in his wake. But that sounds like fancy to me, though the storymakers have picked it up as part of the way they now tell the tale. Still—how could he have seen porpoises in the dark? I suspect they were only the haverings of a hungry, wounded lad, for he had not had a bit of food or drink with him but only some Fisherman's Friend drops he carried for a sore throat. They were all that had sustained him on that wild ride.

Nothing, however, sustained the sea dragon. It ran out of steam by noon of the second day, tried once to stove the little Zulu in, and only succeeded in toppling the already loosened mast. The mast crashed into the sea where the dragon was lying on its side, exhausted, its ruined eye staring blindly up into the brilliant, cloudless blue sky. Mast hit hook and hammered it with one blow straight into the beast's brain. And there the sea dragon died, a hundred nautical miles from land.

By the time Robert had rowed the little boat home, towing the great carcass behind him, it was a day and a half later. A truly impressive feat. He had been aided by some good winds and a fair tide. But he'd had no mast and no sail to take full advantage. It was desperate work. Only about half the creature remained intact; the sea has its own jackals.

The entire town—all who had turned out to talk of his funeral just two days before and more—came out to greet him in their boats. He was a rare hero, the best of Anster, the best of the entire East Neuk.

When Robert finally reached land, his father grabbed his hand and held it, tears running down the old man's cheeks. His mother took him by the shoulders and shook him until they were both red in the face. And then she saw the scabs on his palms, and pulling up the legs of his trousers, saw the scabs on his legs. At that, she threw her arms around him and hugged him until they were both breathless and worn. But none of them said a word the whole time. The McLeods are not much for conversation.

Reverend Dougal used that ride as the topic for a month of sermons, each one longer than the last. No one slept a wink at the kirk services, for fear of missing a word of the story.

And what was left of the beast, Annie McLeod salted down. It filled seventeen full barrels and one neat little firkin. Sea dragon tastes a bit like herring cooked on an open fire, only slightly sharper. It was so much in demand, she traded most of the barrels for tatties and neaps, enough to keep the McLeods full and hearty for years to come.

As for young Robert, after that ride he'd enough of the sea to last him a lifetime. He moved to St. Andrews and apprenticed to a blacksmith. He made hooks. Lots of hooks. All of good cold iron.

I understand they are quite the best in all of Britain for killing monsters, on land or under the sea.

Wilding

ENA BOUNCED down the brownstone steps two at a time, her face powdered a light green. It was the latest color and though she didn't think she looked particularly good in it, all the girls were wearing it. Her nails were striped the same hue. She had good nails.

"Zen!" her mother called out the window. "Where are you going? Have you finished your homework?"

"Yes, Mom," Zena said without turning around. "I finished." *Well, almost,* she thought.

"And where are you—"

This time Zena turned. "Out!"

"Out where?"

Ever since Mom had separated from her third pairing, she had been overzealous in her questioning. *Where are you going? What are you doing? Who's going with you?* Zena hated all the questions, hated the old nicknames. Zen. Princess. Little Bit.

"Just out."

"Princess, just tell me where. So I won't have to worry."

"We're just going Wilding," Zena said, begrudging each syllable.

"I wish you wouldn't. That's the third time this month. It's not...not good. It's dangerous. There have been...deaths."

"That's gus, Mom. As in bo-gus. Ganda. As in propaganda. And you know it."

"It was on the news."

Zena made a face but didn't deign to answer. Everyone knew the news was not to be trusted.

"Don't forget your collar, then."

Zena pulled the collar out of her coat pocket and held it up above her head as she went down the last of the steps. She waggled it at the window. *That*, she thought, *should quiet Mom's nagging.* Not that she planned to wear the collar. Collars were for little kids out on their first Wildings. Or for tourist woggers. What did she need with one? She was already sixteen and, as the Pack's song went:

> *Sweet sixteen*
> *Powdered green*
> *Out in the park*
> *Well after dark,*
> *Wilding!*

The torpedo train growled its way uptown and Zena stood, legs wide apart, disdaining the handgrips. *Hangers are for tourist woggers,* she thought, watching as a pair of high-heeled out-of-towners clutched the overhead straps so tightly their hands turned white from blood loss.

The numbers flashed by—72, 85, 96. She bent her knees and straightened just in time for the torp to jar to a stop and disgorge its passengers. The woggers, hand-combing their dye jobs, got off, too. Zena refused to look at them but guessed they were going where she was going—to the Entrance.

Central Park's walls were now seventeen feet high and topped with electronic mesh. There were only two entrances, built when Wilding became legal. The Westside Entrance was for going in. The Fifty-ninth Eastside was for going out.

As she came up the steps into the pearly evening light, Zena blinked. First Church was gleaming white and the incised letters on its facade were the only reminder of its religious past. The banners now hanging from its door proclaimed WILD WOOD CENTRAL, and the fluttering wolf and tiger flags, symbols of extinct mammals, gave a fair indication of the wind. Right now wind meant little to her, but once she was Wilding, she would know every nuance of it.

Zena sniffed the air. Good wind meant good tracking. If she went predator. She smiled in anticipation.

Behind her she could hear the *tip-taps* of wogger high heels. The woggers were giggling, a little scared. *Well,* Zena thought, *they should be a little scared. Wilding is a pure New York sport. No mushy woggers need apply.*

She stepped quickly up the marble steps and entered the mammoth hall.

PRINT HERE, sang out the first display. Zena put her hand on the screen and it read her quickly. She knew she didn't have to worry. Her record was clear—no drugs, no drags. And her mom kept her creddies high enough. Not like some kids who got turned back everywhere, even off the torp trains. And the third time, a dark black line got printed across their palms. A month's worth of indelible ink. *Indelis* meant a month full of no: no vids, no torp trains, no boo-ti-ques for clothes. And no Wilding. *How,* Zena wondered, *could they stand it?*

Nick was waiting by the Wild Wood Central outdoor. He was talking to Marnie and a good-looking dark-haired guy who Marnie was leaning against familiarly.

"Whizzard!" Nick called out when he saw Zena, and she almost blushed under the green powder. Just the one word, said with appreciation, but otherwise he didn't blink a lash. Zena liked that about Nick. There was something coolish, something even statue about him. And something dangerous, too, even outside the park, outside of Wilding. It was why they were seeing each other, though even after three months, Zena had never, would never, bring him home to meet her mother.

That dangerousness. Zena had it, too.

She went over and started to apologize for being late, saw the shuttered look in Nick's eyes, and changed her apology into an amusing story about her mom instead. She remembered Nick had once said, *Apologies are for woggers and kids.*

From her leaning position, Marnie introduced the dark-haired guy as Lazlo. He had dark eyes, too, the rims slightly yellow, which gave him a disquieting appearance. He grunted a hello.

Zena nodded. To do more would have been uncoolish.

"Like the mean green," Marnie said. "Looks cool-ish on you, foolish on me."

"Na-na," Zena answered, which was what she was supposed to answer. And, actually, she did think Marnie looked good in the green.

"Then let's go Wilding," Marnie said, putting on her collar.

Nick sniffed disdainfully, but he turned toward the door.

The four of them walked out through the tunnel, Marnie and Lazlo holding hands, even though Zena knew he was a just-met. She and Marnie knew everything about one another, had since preschool. Still, that was just like Marnie, overeager in everything.

Nick walked along in his low, slow, almost

boneless way that made Zena want to sigh out loud, but she didn't. Soundless, she strode along by his side, their shoulders almost—but not quite—touching. The small bit of air between them crackled with a hot intensity.

As they passed through the first set of rays, a dull yellow light bathed their faces. Zena felt the first shudder go through her body but she worked to control it. In front of her, Lazlo's whole frame seemed to shake.

"Virg," Nick whispered to her, meaning it was Lazlo's first time out Wilding.

Zena was surprised. "True?" she asked.

"He's from O-Hi," Nick said. Then, almost as an afterthought, added, "My cousin."

"O-Hi?" Zena said, smothering both the surprise in her voice and the desire to giggle. Neither would have been coolish. She hadn't known Nick had any cousins, let alone from O-Hi—the boons, the breads of America. No one left O-Hi except as a tourist. And woggers just didn't look like Lazlo. Nick must have dressed him, must have lent him clothes, must have cut his hair in its fine duo-bop, one side long to the shoulder, one side shaved clean. Zena wondered if Marnie knew Lazlo was from O-Hi. Or if she cared. *Maybe,* Zena thought suddenly, *maybe I don't know Marnie as well as I thought I did.*

They passed the second set of rays; the light was blood red. She felt the beginnings of the change. It was not exactly unpleasant, either. *Something to do*, she remembered from the Wilding brochures she had read back when she was a kid, *with manipulating the basic DNA for a couple of hours.* She'd never really understood that sort of thing. She was suddenly reminded of the first time she'd come to Wild Wood Central, with a bunch of her girlfriends. Not coolish, of course, just giggly girls. None of them had stayed past dark and none had been greatly changed that time. Just a bit of hair, a bit of fang. Only Ginger had gotten a tail. But then she was the only one who'd hit puberty early; it ran in Ginger's family. Zena and her friends had all gone screaming through the park as fast as they could, and they'd all been wearing collars. Collars made the transition back to human easy, needing no effort on their parts, no will.

Zena reached into the pocket of her coat, fingering the leather collar there. She had plenty of will without it. *Plenty of won't, too!* she thought, feeling a bubble of amusement rise inside. *Will/won't. Will/won't.* The sound bumped about in her head.

When they passed the third rays, the deep green ones, which made her green face powder sparkle and spread in a mask, Zena laughed out loud. Green rays always seemed to tickle her. Her laugh was high, uncontrolled. Marnie was laughing as well, chittering almost. The green rays took her that way, too. But the boys both gave deep, dark grunts. Lazlo sounded just like Nick.

The brown rays caught them all in the middle of

changing and—too late—Zena thought about the collar again. Marnie was wearing hers, and Lazlo his. When she turned to check on Nick, all she saw was a flash of yellow teeth and yellow eyes. For some reason, that so frightened her, she skittered collarless through the tunnel ahead of them all and was gone, Wilding.

The park was a dark, trembling, mysterious green; a pulsating, moist jungle where leaves large as platters reached out with their bitter, prickly auricles. Monkshood and stagbush, sticklewort and sumac stung Zena's legs as she ran twisting and turning along the pathways, heading toward the open meadow and the fading light, her new tail curled up over her back.

She thought she heard her name being called, but when she turned her head to call back, the only sounds out of her mouth were the pipings and chitterings of a beast. Still, the collar had been in her pocket, and the clothes, molded into monkey skin, remained close enough to her to lend her some human memories. Not as strong as if she had been collared, but strong enough.

She forced herself to stop running, forced herself back to a kind of calm. She could feel her human instincts fighting with her monkey memories. The monkey self—not predator but prey—screamed, *Hide! Run! Hide!* The human self reminded her that it was all a game, all in fun.

She trotted toward the meadow, safe in the

knowledge that the creepier animals favored the moist, dark tunnel-like passages under the heavy canopy of leaves.

However, by the time she got to the meadow, scampering the last hundred yards on all fours, the daylight was nearly gone. It was, after all, past seven. Maybe even close to eight. It was difficult to tell time in the park.

There was one slim whitish tree at the edge of the meadow. Birch, her human self named it. She climbed it quickly, monkey fingers lending her speed and agility. Near the top, where the tree got bendy, she stopped to scan the meadow. It was aboil with creatures, some partly human, some purely beast. Occasionally one would leap high above the long grass, screeching. It was unclear from the sound whether it was a scream of fear or laughter.

And then she stopped thinking human thoughts at all, surrendering entirely to the Wilding. Smells assaulted her—the sharp tang of leaves, the mustier trunk smell, a sweet larva scent. Her long fingers tore at the bark, uncovering a scramble of beetles. She plucked them up, crammed them into her mouth, tasting the gingery snap of the shells.

A howl beneath the tree made her shiver. She stared down into a black mouth filled with yellow teeth.

"Hunger! Hunger!" howled the mouth.

She scrambled higher up into the tree, which

began to shake dangerously and bend with her weight. Above, a pale, thin moon was rising. She reached one hand up, tried to pluck the moon as if it were a piece of fruit, using her tail for balance. When her fingers closed on nothing, she chittered unhappily. By her third attempt she was tired of the game and, seeing no danger lingering at the tree's base, climbed down.

The meadow grass was high, and tickled as she ran. Near her, others were scampering, but none reeked of predator and she moved rapidly alongside them, all heading in one direction—toward the smell of water.

The water was in a murky stream. Reaching it, she bent over and drank directly, lapping and sipping in equal measure. The water was cold and sour with urine. She spit it out and looked up. On the other side of the stream was a small copse of trees.

Trees! sang out her monkey mind.

However, she would not wade through the water. Finding a series of rocks, she jumped eagerly stone-to-stone-to-stone. When she got to the other side, she shook her hands and feet vigorously, then gave her tail a shake as well. She did not like the feel of the water. When she was dry enough, she headed for the trees.

At the foot of one tree was a body, human, but crumpled as if it were a pile of old clothes. Green face paint mixed with blood. She touched the leg, then the shoulder, and whimpered. A name came to her. *Mamie?* Then it faded. She touched the unfamiliar face. It was still warm, blood still flowing. Somewhere in the back part of her mind, the human part, she knew she should be doing something. But *what* seemed muddled and far away. She sat by the side of the body, shivering uncontrollably, will-less.

Suddenly there was a deep, low growl behind her and she leaped up, all unthinking, and headed toward the tree. Something caught her tail and pulled. She screamed, high, piercing. And then knifing through her mind, sharp and keen, was a human thought. *Fight.* She turned and kicked out at whatever had hold of her.

All she could see was a dark face with a wide hole for a mouth, and staring blue eyes. Then the creature was on top of her and all her kicking did not seem to be able to stop it at all.

The black face was so close she could smell its breath, hot and carnal. With one final human effort, she reached up to scratch the face and was startled because it did not feel at all like flesh. *Mask,* her human mind said, and then all her human senses flooded back. The park was suddenly less close, less alive. Sounds once so clear were muddied. Smells faded. But she knew what to do about her attacker. She ripped the mask from his face.

He blinked his blue eyes in surprise, his pale face splotchy with anger. For a moment he was stunned, watching her change beneath him, no longer a monkey, now a strong girl. A strong, screaming girl. She kicked again, straight up.

This time he was the one to scream.

It was all the screaming, not her kicking, that saved her. Suddenly there were a half-dozen men in camouflage around her. Men—not animals. She could scarcely understand where they'd come from. But they grabbed her attacker and carried him off. Only two of them stayed with her until the ambulance arrived.

"I don't get it," Zena said when at last she could sit up in the hospital bed. She ached everywhere, but she was alive.

"Without your collar," the man by her bedside said, "it's almost impossible to flash back to being human. You'd normally have had to wait out the entire five hours of Wilding. No shortcuts back."

"I know that," Zena said. It came out sharper than she meant, so she added, "I know you, too. You were one of my...rescuers."

He nodded. "You were lucky. Usually only the dead flash back that fast."

"So that's what happened to that..."

"Her name was Sandra Maharish."

"Oh."

"She'd been foolish enough to leave off her collar, too. Only she hadn't the will you have, the will to flash and fight. It's what saved you."

Zena's mind went, *Will/won't. Will/won't.*

"What?" the man asked. Evidently she had said it aloud.

"Will," Zena whispered. "Only I didn't save me. You did."

"No, Zena, we could never have gotten to you in time if you hadn't screamed. Without the collar, Wild Wood Central can't track you. He counted on that."

"Track me?" Zena, unthinking, put a hand to her neck, found a bandage there.

"We try to keep a careful accounting of everything that goes on in the park," the man said. He looked, Zena thought, pretty coolish in his camouflage. Interesting looking, too, his face all planes and angles, with a wild, brushy orange mustache. Almost like one of those old pirates.

"Why?" she asked.

"Now that the city is safe everywhere else, people go Wilding just to feel that little shiver of fear. Just to get in touch with their primal selves."

" 'Mime the prime,' " Zena said, remembering one of the old commercials.

"Exactly." He smiled. It was a very coolish smile. "And it's our job to make that fear safe. Control the chaos. Keep prime time clean."

"Then that guy..." Zena began, shuddering as she recalled the black mask, the hands around her neck.

"He'd actually killed three other girls, the Maharish girl being his latest. All girls without their collars who didn't have the human fight-back knowhow. He'd gotten in unchanged through one of the old tunnels that we should have had blocked. 'Those wild girls,' he called his victims. Thanks to you, we caught him."

"Are you a cop?" Zena wrinkled her nose a bit.

"Nope. I'm a Max," he said, giving her a long, slow wink.

"A Max?"

"We control the Wild Things!" When she looked blank, he said, "It's an old story." He handed her a card. "In case you want to know more."

Zena looked at the card. It was embellished with holograms, front and back, of extinct animals. His name, Carl Barkham, was emblazoned in red across the elephant.

Just then her mother came in. Barkham greeted her with a mock salute and left. He walked down the hall with a deliberate, rangy stride that made him look, Zena thought, a lot like a powerful animal. A lion. Or a tiger.

"Princess!" her mother cried. "I came as soon as I heard."

"I'm fine, Mom," Zena said, not even wincing at the old nickname.

Behind her were Marnie, Lazlo, and Nick. They stood silently by the bed. At last Nick whispered, "You OK?" Somehow he seemed small, young, boneless. He was glancing nervously at Zena, at her mother, then back again. It was very uncoolish.

"I'm fine," Zena said. "Just a little achey." If Barkham was a tiger, then Nick was just a cub. "But I realize now that going collarless was really dumb. I was plain lucky."

"Coolish," Nick said.

But it wasn't. The Max was coolish. Nick was just...just...foolish.

"I'm ready to go home, Mom," Zena said. "I've got a lot of homework."

"Homework?" The word fell out of Nick's slack mouth.

She smiled pityingly at him, put her feet over the side of the bed, and stood. "I've got a lot of studying to do if I want to become a Max."

"What's a Max?" all four of them asked at once.

"Someone who tames the Wild Things," she said. "It's an old story. Come on, Mom. I'm starving. Got anything still hot for dinner?"

The
Baby-Sitter

ILARY HATED BABY-SITTING at the
Mitchells' house, though she loved the
Mitchell twins. The house was one of those
old, creaky Victorian horrors, with a dozen rooms
and two sets of stairs. One set led from the front hall,
and one, which the servants had used back in the
1890s, led up from the kitchen.

There was a long, dark hallway upstairs, and the
twins slept at the end of it. Each time Hilary checked
on them, she felt as if there were things watching her
from behind the closed doors of the other rooms or
from the walls. She couldn't say what exactly, just
things.

"Do this," Adam Mitchell had said to her the first
time she'd taken them up to bed. He touched one
door with his right hand, the next with his left, spun
around twice on his right leg, then kissed his fingers
one after another. He repeated this ritual three times

down the hall to the room he shared with his brother, Andrew.

> *Once a night,*
> *And you're all right,*

he sang in a Munchkin voice.

Andrew did the same.

Hilary laughed at their antics. They looked so cute, like a pair of six-year-old wizards or pale Michael Jackson clones, she couldn't decide which.

"You do it, Hilary," they urged.

"There's no music, guys," she said. "And I don't dance without music."

"But it's not dancing, Hilly," Adam said. "It's magic."

"It keeps Them away," Andrew added. "We don't like Them. Grandma showed us how. This was her house first. And her grandmother's before her. If you do it, They won't bother you."

"Well, don't worry about Them," Hilary said. "Or anything else. That's what I'm hired for, to make sure nothing bad happens to you while your mom and dad are out."

But her promises hadn't satisfied them, and in the end, to keep them happy, she banged on each door and spun around on her right leg, and kissed her fingers, too. It was a lot of fun, actually. She had taught it to her best friend, Brenda, the next day in school, and pretty soon half the kids in the ninth grade had picked it up. They called it the Mitchell March, but secretly Hilary called it the Spell.

The first night's baby-sitting, after they had danced the Spell all the way down the long hall, Hilary had tucked the boys into their beds and pulled up a rocking chair between. Then she told them stories for almost an hour until first Adam and then Andrew fell asleep. In one night she'd become their favorite baby-sitter.

She had told them baby stories that time—"The Three Bears" and "The Three Billy Goats Gruff" and "The Three Little Pigs," all with sound effects and a different voice for each character. After that she relied on TV plots and the books she'd read in school for her material. Luckily she was a great reader.

The twins hated to ever hear a story a second time. Except for "The Golden Arm," the jump story that she'd learned on a camping trip when she was nine. Adam and Andrew asked for *that* one every time.

When she had asked them why, Adam had replied solemnly, his green eyes wide, "Because it scares Them."

After she smoothed the covers over the sleeping boys, Hilary always drew in a deep breath before heading down the long, uncarpeted hall. It didn't matter which stairs she headed for, there was always a strange echo as she walked along, each footstep articulated with precision, and then a slight *tap-tapping* afterward. She never failed to turn around after the first few steps. She never saw anything behind her.

The Mitchells called her at least three times a month, and though she always hesitated to accept, she always went. Part of it was she really loved the twins. They were bright, polite, and funny in equal measure. And they were not shy about telling her how much they liked her. But there was something else, too. Hilary was a stubborn girl. You couldn't tell from the set of her jaw; she had a sweet, rounded jaw. And her nose was too snubbed to be taken seriously. But when she thought someone was treating her badly or trying to threaten her, she always dug in and made a fuss.

Like the time the school principal had tried to ban miniskirts and had sent Brenda home for wearing one. Hilary had changed into her junior varsity cheerleading uniform and walked into Mr. Golden's office.

"Do you like our uniforms, sir?" she had said, quietly.

"Of course, Hilary," Mr. Golden had answered, being too sure of himself to know a trap when he was walking into it.

"Well, we represent the school in these uniforms, don't we?" she had asked.

"And you do a wonderful job, too," he said.

Snap. The sound of the closing trap. "Well, they are

shorter than any miniskirt," she said. "And when we do cartwheels, our bloomers show! Brenda never does cartwheels." She'd smiled then, but there was a deep challenge in her eyes.

Mr. Golden rescinded the ban the next day.

So Hilary didn't like the idea that any Them, real or imagined, would make her afraid to sit with her favorite six-year-olds. She always said yes to Mrs. Mitchell in the end.

It was on the night before Halloween, a Sunday, the moon hanging ripely over the Mitchells' front yard, that Hilary went to sit for the twins. Dressed as a wolf in a sheep's clothing, Mr. Mitchell let her in.

"I said they could stay up and watch the Disney special," he said. "It's two hours, and lasts well past their bedtime. But we are making an exception tonight. I hope you don't mind." His sheep ears bobbed.

She had no homework and had just finished reading Shirley Jackson's *The Haunting of Hill House*, which was scary enough for her to prefer having the extra company.

"No problem, Mr. Mitchell," she said.

Mrs. Mitchell came out of the kitchen carrying a pumpkin pie. Her costume was a traditional witch's. A black stringy wig covered her blond hair. She had blackened one of her front teeth. The twins trailed behind her, each eating a cookie.

"Now, no more cookies," Mrs. Mitchell said, more to Hilary than to the boys.

Hilary winked at them. Adam grinned, but Andrew, intent on trying to step on the long black hem of his mother's skirt, missed the wink.

"Good-bye," Hilary called, shutting the door behind the Mitchells. She had a glimpse of the moon, which reminded her of the Jackson book, and made a face at it. Then she turned to the twins. "Now, what about those cookies?" she asked.

They raced to the kitchen, and each had one of the fresh-baked chocolate-chip cookies, the kind with the real runny chocolate.

"Crumbs don't count," Hilary said. She scraped around the dish for the crumbs, and having counted what cookies remained—there were thirteen—she shooed the boys back into the living room. They turned on the TV and settled down to watch the show, sharing the handful of crumbs slowly through the opening credits.

Adam lasted through the first hour but was fast asleep in Hilary's lap before the second. Andrew stayed awake until nearly the end, but his eyes kept closing through the commercials. At the final ad, for vitamins, he fell asleep for good.

Hilary sighed. She would have to carry them upstairs to bed. Since she wanted to watch *Friday the Thirteenth, Part II*—or at least she thought she wanted to watch it—she needed to get them upstairs. It wouldn't do for either one to wake up and be scared by the show. And if she woke them, they'd want to know the end of the Disney movie and hear at least one other story. She would miss her show. So she hoisted Adam in her arms and went up the stairs.

He nuzzled against her shoulder and looked so vulnerable and sweet as she walked down the creaky hall, she smiled. Playfully she touched the doors in the proper order, turning around heavily on one leg. She couldn't quite reach her fingers with her mouth until she dumped him on his bed. After covering him with his quilt, she kissed his forehead and then, with a grin, kissed each of her fingers in turn, whispering, "So there," to the walls when she was done.

She ran down the stairs for Andrew and carried him up as well. He opened his eyes just before they reached the top step.

"Don't forget," he whispered. To placate him, she touched the doors, turned, and kissed her fingers one at a time.

He smiled sleepily and murmured, "All right. All right now."

He was fast asleep when she put him under the covers. She straightened up, watched them both for a moment more, listened to their quiet breathing, and went out of the room.

As she went down the stairs, the hollow *tap-tapping* echo behind her had a furtive sound. She turned quickly but saw nothing. Still, she was happy to be downstairs again.

The first half of the show was scary enough. Hilary sat with her feet tucked under a blanket, arms wrapped around her legs. She liked scary stuff usually. She had seen *Alien* and *Aliens* and even *Jaws* without blanching, and had finished a giant box of popcorn with Brenda at *Night of the Living Dead*. But somehow, watching a scary movie alone in the Mitchells' spooky house was too much. Remembering the popcorn, she thought that eating might help. There were still those thirteen chocolate-chip cookies left. Mrs. Mitchell had meant the boys weren't supposed to eat them. Hilary knew she hadn't meant the baby-sitter to starve.

During the commercial break, she threw off the blanket and padded into the kitchen. Mrs. Mitchell had just had new linoleum put on the floor. With a little run, Hilary slid halfway across in her socks.

The plate of cookies was sitting on the counter, next to the stove. Hilary looked at it strangely. There were no longer thirteen cookies. She counted quickly. Seven—no, eight. Someone had eaten five.

"Those twins!" she said aloud. But she knew it couldn't have been them. They never disobeyed, except when she let them, and their mother had said specifically that they could have no more. Besides, they had never left the sofa once the movie had started. And the only time she had left either one of them alone had been when she had taken Adam upstairs, leaving Andrew asleep.... She stopped. Andrew hadn't been asleep. Not entirely. Still, she couldn't imagine Andrew polishing off five chocolate-chip cookies in the time it had taken her to tuck Adam into bed.

"Now..." she said to herself, "if it had been Dana Jankowitz!" She'd baby-sat Dana for almost a year before they moved away, and that kid was capable of anything.

Still puzzled, she went over to the plate of cookies, and as she got close, she stepped into something cold and wet. She looked down. There was a puddle on the floor, soaking into her right sock. An icy-cold puddle. Hilary looked out the kitchen window. It was raining.

Someone was in the house.

She didn't want to believe it, but there was no other explanation. Her whole body felt cold, and she could feel her heart stuttering in her chest. She thought about the twins sleeping upstairs, how she had told them she was hired to make sure nothing bad happened to them. But what if something bad happened to *her*? She shuddered and looked across the room. The telephone was hanging by the refrigerator. She could try and phone for help, or she could run outside and go to the nearest house. The Mitchells lived down a long driveway, and it was about a quarter mile to the next home. And dark. And wet. And she didn't know how many someones were in the house. Or outside. And maybe it was all her imagination.

But—and if her jaw trembled just the slightest she didn't think anyone could fault her—what if the someones wanted to hurt the twins? She was the only one home to protect them.

As silently as possible, she slid open the knife drawer and took out a long, sharp carving knife. Then slowly she opened the door to the back stairs...

...and the man hiding there leaped at her. His face was hidden behind a gorilla mask. He was at least six feet tall, wearing blue jeans and a green shirt. She was so frightened she dropped the knife and ran through the dining room, into the living room, and up the front stairs.

Calling, "Girly, girly, girly, come here," the man ran after her.

Hilary took the steps two at a time, shot around the corner, and ran down the hall. If only she could get to the twins' room, she thought, she could lock and barricade the door by pushing the dressers in front of it. And then she'd wake up the twins and they'd go through the trapdoor in the closet up to the attic. They'd be safe there.

But the man was pounding behind her, laughing oddly and calling out.

Hilary heard the chittering only after she passed

the third door. And the man's screaming as she got to the twins' room. She didn't take time to look behind her but slid into the room, slammed the door, rammed the bolt home, and slipped the desk chair under the doorknob. She didn't bother waking the twins or moving anything else in front of the door. The man's high screams subsided to a low, horrifying moan. Then at last they stopped altogether. After all, he hadn't taken time to touch the doors or turn on his leg or kiss his fingers one at a time. He hadn't known the warding spell. *Once a night and you're...*

She waited a long time before opening the door and peeking out. When she did, all she could see was a crumpled gorilla mask, a piece out of a green shirt, and a dark stain on the floor that was rapidly disappearing, as if someone—or something—were licking it up.

Hilary closed the door quietly. She took a deep breath and lay down on top of the covers by Andrew's side. Next time she came to baby-sit, she wouldn't tell the "Golden Arm" story. Not next time or ever. After all, she owed *Them* a favor.

Bolundeers

THE ONE CHORE Brancy hated more than any other was taking out the food scraps and emptying them into the compost heap. She didn't mind the dry garbage, or rinsing out the bottles and cans for the recycling bins. She didn't even mind tying up the endless numbers of newspapers that seemed to positively breed in her mother's den, though she refused to go into the den to get them. But the compost...

She flung the final bucketload onto the small mountain of scraps and tried not to watch the tomato ends and eggshells creep down the slimy sides. And she didn't take a new breath until she was well upwind and moving fast.

God! she thought. Then amended it quickly, in case God was listening, though she doubted he was. *Gosh!* Ever since her father's death she had had these big moments of Unbelief. *Still,* she thought, *probably better not to swear.* She had an additional thought then. *Imagine if the whole world was like the compost heap. And not just my life.*

Of course, the world had once actually been that way. They had talked about that in school. The Cretaceous, with its great, wet, green, muddy, mucky, swamp-and-romp dinosaur playground. It was supposed to have been full of fetid and moist, murky growth. Like an overgrown compost heap. *Imagine living in that!* Brancy thought. *I'd rather die first.*

The word *die* resounded inside her. It was ugly and sharp and it hurt.

She rinsed the pail at the outside tap, then walked back into the house. "Done," she called out to her little brother. "I get dishes tomorrow, and you, Mr. Brat—you get the compost."

"I hate the compost," Danny whimpered. "Something's growing out there." He spoke in the quiet, whispery, scared voice he had used ever since their father died.

"Of course something's growing there," Brancy said. She deliberately made her voice sound spooky.

"It is?" His eyes got wide.

"Volunteers," Brancy told him. "And if you're not careful, they'll get you!"

"Mommmmmmmy," Danny cried, and ran out of the room.

Moments later he came back, followed by their mother. She was not amused. "Brancy, he has had enough nightmares since...without you adding to them." Her mother never actually used the word *death*. Or *cancer*. Her conversation was full of odd ellipses and gaps. Brancy hated it. "I need you to be more...understanding about...about things."

"All I said was that volunteers grow up in the compost heap. And you know they do."

"She said the Bolundeers would get me." Danny was white faced. "Maybe get all of us. Like they got..." He didn't say the word *Daddy*. He didn't have to.

Mrs. Callanish knelt down. "Oh, Danny, a *volunteer*"—she pronounced the word very carefully—"is a tomato or squash or some other vegetable that grows from the seeds that are thrown into the compost heap. And they can't possibly get you. Not like... Have you ever seen a fierce tomato or a mean pumpkin?" She made a face.

"At Halloween," Brancy said. "All those teeth."

"Brancy!" Mrs. Callanish's mouth was drawn down into a thin line.

Brancy knew, even before her mother spoke, that she had gone too far this time. In fact, since her father's death everything that Brancy said or did seemed wrong, hurtful, awry.

Her mother was changed, too, beyond all recognition. Before, she had been a funny, cozy kind of mom, always ready to listen, even when she was busy. And as a DA, she was always busy. Now she was stern and unreachable. Brancy understood why—or thought she did. Her mother was trying to be brave and strong, like her father had been throughout his illness. But what made everything worse was that her mother never let them talk about him. About his illness, about his death. She just set his memory firmly between the spaces. He was... (gone).... It was almost as though he had never been a part of their lives at all.

"OK, get your homework out of the way and then we can have a chapter of Tolkien tonight. I've managed to get most of my work done." Mrs. Callanish nodded, but there was no warmth in her voice, as if reading to them were a duty she was still willing to perform—but not one she was happy doing.

Brancy knew that Danny would be finished with his homework first. After all, how much homework does a kindergartner have, except maybe coloring? But she had at least an hour of math and social studies and a whole page of spelling words to memorize. Mr. Dooley, her English teacher, was a bear on spelling words. He had won a national spelling bee as a fourth grader and loved to tell them about it. Before her father had died, Brancy had been class champion— and Mr. Dooley's pet. But she had gotten C's on her last three spelling tests and had never made up the two she missed because of the funeral. Mr. Dooley didn't even kid around with her anymore. *Which is fine,* Brancy thought. *Just fine. Mr. Dooley is kind of goofy on the subject of spelling, anyway.*

It turned out to be more like three hours of homework, though—one before the Tolkien, and two after—and Brancy was exhausted. Eighth grade was going to be real hard, she decided. The spelling words had been the worst ever: *naiad, Gorgon, nemesis, daimonic, centaur, odyssey.* They were studying the myths of ancient worlds. Brancy wished the ancient worlds had known how to spell with more regularity. Or had had fewer odd gods and monsters.

"Though how anyone could *really* believe in this stuff..." she said, slamming the book shut. "It's all too bizarre."

"Brancy," came a whispery voice from the door connecting her bedroom with Danny's.

She looked up. Danny was standing there, holding on to his bear, Bronco.

"Hey, Mr. Brat, it's way past ten. What are you doing up?"

"I heard the Bolundeers outside. In the compost." His chin trembled. "They're scratching around. And whispering awful things about you and me and Mom. They want to come into the house. Listen."

She listened. All she could hear were crickets. "You know what Mom said. *Volunteers*"—she pronounced it again carefully—"are vegetables. And vegetables don't make any noise. In fact, they are very very quiet."

"Not these ones," Danny said. "These are Bolundeers. They want to hurt us. Brancy, I'm scared."

She started to say something sharp but his face was so pinched and white that she bit back the response. He hardly looked like a kindergartner anymore. In fact, he looked like a little old man. A little old *dying* man. "Do you want me to snuggle with you till you fall asleep?"

He nodded, clutching Bronco so hard the little bear's eyes almost popped out.

"OK. I was getting tired of Gorgons and centaurs, anyway."

"What are those?"

"Far worse than talking veggies, trust me." She followed him back to his bed. Tucking in next to him, she said, "Why don't I sing you something?" He nodded, and so she started with their father's favorite lullaby, the one he always sang when they were sick and couldn't fall asleep: "Dance to Your Daddy." Only, unlike their father, she sang it on key.

Danny dozed off at once, but Brancy could not sleep. The song only served to remind her that her father was no longer around. He had suffered horribly before finally dying, and God had been no help to him at all. Even though they had all prayed and his partner had had a mass said for him. It didn't matter that her father had been strong and brave before he had gotten cancer. With medals from the city after having been injured in the line of duty. He hadn't died when some man crazy with drugs had tried to kill him with a knife. Or later, when he had shielded two hostages with his own body while a would-be burglar had shot at them. It was stupid lung cancer from his stupid smoking that had killed him. She tried to remember what her father had looked like, either before the cancer or after. But all that came to mind was what they had left of him, in a jar on a shelf in her mother's den.

Ashes.

Morning was dirty and gray as an erased blackboard. Brancy got up from her brother's bed, where she had slept fitfully, on top of the covers. She brushed her teeth quickly, ran her fingers through her short hair, and got dressed with a lack of enthusiasm. The other girls in her class, she knew, made dressing the long, important focus of their day. But ever since...She stopped herself. Then, afraid that she was beginning to sound like her mother, she said aloud, "Ever since Daddy died..." Well, clothes and things weren't so important anymore. Or school.

In fact, Brancy was so tired, she dozed through most of her classes. She was all but sleepwalking when she picked up Danny from afternoon kindergarten. Still, she was awake enough to see that his pinched-old-man look was gone, and she smiled at him. Hand-in-hand they walked back toward home, with Danny babbling on and on about stuff in a normal tone. Only, when they turned the corner of Prospect Street, he was suddenly silent and his face was the gray-white of old snow.

"Cat got your tongue, Mr. Brat?" Brancy asked.

"Do you think..." he whispered, "that the Bolundeers will be waiting for us?"

"Oh, Danny!" Brancy answered, unable to keep the exasperation in her voice hidden. She was too tired for that. "Mom explained. I explained." She shook her head at him. But his hand in hers was damp.

"Don't let them get me, Brancy," he said. "Don't let them hurt me. I'm not brave like Daddy."

She dropped his hand and knelt down in front of him so they were eye-to-eye. "No one," she said forcefully, "is going to hurt you. Not while I'm around."

"Daddy got hurt." His eyes teared up.

She dropped her books to the ground and put her arms around him. She couldn't think of anything to say. And besides, their mother didn't want them to talk about it. She found herself snuffling, and Danny pulled away.

"Don't cry, Brancy," he said.

"I'm not crying. I've got a rain cloud in my eyes." It was something their father used to say.

"Oh, Brancy!" Danny was suddenly bright again, as if he had forgotten all about his fears. He took her hand. "I think we need to go home now."

And they did. Straight home. Without talking.

Brancy did her homework in the living room, to keep an eye on Danny while he watched television. But she was so engrossed in the reading she didn't notice when he left the room in between commercials. When she realized he was gone, she got up, stretched, and went to look for him.

He wasn't downstairs, and she raced up the stairs to see if he was—for some reason—in the bedrooms. Sometimes, she knew, a five-year-old could get into a lot of trouble by himself. But he wasn't upstairs, either. She was close to panic when she glanced out the bedroom window and saw him by the compost heap. What he was doing there was so shocking, she screamed. Then she ran down the stairs and outside, without taking time to put her shoes on. The grass soaked her socks.

"Danny!" she cried. "Stop! Oh, Danny. What have you done?"

He turned to her, smiling. "Daddy will take care of those Bolundeers all right. Just like he takes care of all the bad guys."

She took the urn from him and looked in. It was totally empty. She didn't dare stare over his shoulder into the compost heap, where she knew the gray ashes would already be settling into the slime. "Oh, Danny," she whispered, "we can't tell Mommy. We just can't."

And they didn't. Not at dinner, and not at bed-time. Danny because he'd promised Brancy, and he did not know exactly what was wrong. And Brancy because she did know. Exactly.

That night, as she lay in her bed, Brancy heard the sound Danny must have been listening to the night before. The crickets, of course. But underneath their insistent high-pitched chirrupings, something else. Something odd and ugly, scratching and scrabbling across the grass. It sounded awkward and eager, as if it had gained strength before judgment, as if it were hungry, as if it were heading toward the house.

Brancy got up and looked out of the window, but she couldn't see anything out there. Except a series of strange flat black shapes that seemed to hunch and bunch through the grass. But the moon was full and the lawn was covered with shadows. Surely that was what she was seeing.

She shut her window as quietly as possible and pulled down the shade. Then she crept into Danny's room, her heart thudding so loudly she thought it would wake her mother down the hall.

Danny was clutching his bear as if he were frightened, but he was fast asleep. Brancy lay down next to him, afraid to think, afraid to move again, afraid to breathe.

The strange scratching, scrabbling sound seemed to come closer, reaching below Danny's window. Brancy forced herself to get up, to go over to the window and shut it. It slammed down on the sill with a loud whack as sharp as gunshot. But not before Brancy saw the shadows rising up, like some sort of anonymous and deadly gang, their shadowy fingers pointing at her, their shadowy mouths calling in voices as soft and persuasive as dreams. "Danny... we're coming for you next!"

"No!" she cried out loud, "not Danny." She flung herself back onto the bed, setting herself over Danny to protect him. She could feel him breathing beneath her, gentle and trusting; her own breathing was a harsh rasp.

And then she heard something else. It was faint, so faint that at first she thought she was only wishing it. But it got louder, as if whatever made that particular noise had come closer, or had gained its own particular strength from her. It was—she thought— a sound that was strangely off-key. But she recognized it. It was a song, and she sang along with it, quietly at the beginning, then with growing gusto: "Dance to your daddy, my little laddy..."

Danny stirred in his sleep and nuzzled the bear.

"Brancy?" Her mother's voice floated down the hall.

Brancy stopped singing just long enough to call back: "Under control, Mom."

The song seemed to catch up with the eager scratching, then overtake it. There was a moment of strange cacophony, like some kind of grunge band suddenly playing beneath their window.

And then, as if it had been a vine cut down, the scratching stopped.

Slowly the off-key song faded away, and all she could hear then were the ever-present crickets and the faraway hooting of a screech owl, like a lost child crying in the distance.

Brancy got up, went to the window, and slowly

raised it. The air was soft and a shred of cloud covered the full moon. She thought it might soon rain.

"I love you, Daddy," Brancy whispered to the lawn and, beyond it, the compost heap. Then she closed her eyes, which had rain-clouded over with tears. "I miss you." She went back to her own bedroom and lay down on the bed. A minute later she felt someone lift the covers up and over her and hum a bit of an off-key tune.

She didn't open her eyes to see who it was.

She didn't have to.

The next morning at breakfast, Mrs. Callanish stood by the table looking stern, the urn in her arms.

Brancy started to say something, but her mother shook her head.

"I had the most amazing dream last night," she said. "About your...father." She took a deep breath. "I've been wrong to keep his ashes hidden in my den. To make a shrine of them. To forbid you to talk about him and how he died."

Brancy took a deep breath, this time determined to confess what had happened.

But her mother continued talking. "Let's go and spread the ashes in the garden. It was his favorite place. He'll like being there."

"But..." Brancy began, then she looked over at Danny. He was smiling. It was a secret, knowing kind of smile.

Suddenly she understood. The ashes—which she had seen him shake out onto the compost heap—were somehow back in the urn. And then she remembered the soft touch of the shadowy hand on her covers, the soft off-key humming above her bed.

"We can sing Daddy's song while we do it," Danny said. "About dancing."

"I didn't know you knew it," Mrs. Callanish said.

"I know it all," Danny said.

"And what you forget," Brancy added, "I'll remember."

The Bridge's Complaint

Trit-trot, trit-trot, trit-trot, all day long. You'd think their demned hooves were made of iron. It fair gives me a headache, it does. Back and forth, back and forth. As if the grass were actually greener on one side one day, on the other the next. Goats really are a monstrous race.

It makes me long for the days of Troll.

We never were on more than a generic-name basis. He was Troll. I was Bridge. It takes trolls—and bridges, for that matter—a long time to warm up to full introductions. So I never had a chance to know his first name before he was...well...gone. But he was a pleasant sort, for a troll. Knew a lot of stories. Troll stories, of course, are full of blood and food, food and blood. But they were good stories, for all that. Told loudly and with great passion. I really do miss them.

Not that I don't have a few good stories of my

own to tell. I mean, I wasn't always a Goat Bridge. Long before that demned tribe arrived to foul my planking, I was a Bridge of Some Consequence. Mme. d'Aulnoy herself traversed my boards. And her friend Mme. le Prince du Beaumont. Ah—the sound of wheels rolling. There is a memory to treasure.

None of this trit-trot, trit-trot business.

But then the dear ladies were gone and the meadows, once pied with colorful flowers, were sold to a goat merchant, M. de Gruff. He pastured his demned beasties on both sides of my river. They sharpened their horns on my railings, pawed deep into the earthen slopes, and ate up every last one of the flowers. The grass in the meadows was gnawed down to nubbins by those voracious creatures. In other words, they made a desert out of an Eden.

Trit-trot, trit-trot, indeed.

So you can imagine how thrilled I was when Troll showed up, pushing his way upstream from the confluence of the great rivers below.

He wasn't much to look at when he arrived, being young and quite thin. Of course he had the big bran-muffin eyes and the sled-jump nose and the gingko-leaf ears that identify a troll immediately. And when he smiled, there were those moss green teeth, filed to points. But otherwise he was a quite unprepossessing troll.

Trolls are territorial, you know, and when food gets scarce, the young are pushed out by the older, bigger, meaner trolls. Or so my Troll told me, and I have no reason to disbelieve him. He said, "Me dad gave a shove when he got hungry. I had to go. Been on the move awhile."

That was an understatement. Actually he had been wading through miles of river before he found me unoccupied. He must have thought it paradise when he saw all those goats.

Not that he could have run across the fields after them. It is a well-kept secret that trolls must have one foot in the water at all times. Troll told me this one night when we were trading tales. They call it *water-logging*. Troll even sang me a song about it that went something like this:

> Two feet wet,
> None on shore,
> You will live
> Evermore.
>
> One foot wet,
> One foot dry,
> You will never
> Need to cry.
>
> Two feet dry—
> Say good-bye.

Well, trolls are actually better at stories than poems. You want good poetry, you have to hang out with boggles or sprites.

Of course the whole thing is a secret and I only tell you this because there are no longer many trolls about. It is a shame, actually. M. Darwin wrote of this disappearing phenomenon, and I, for one, believe it.

So trolls must wait by a river's bank for some creature to cross if they want to eat. That's why trolls and bridges have such an affinity. A bridge means a crossing place, and we are much more stable than fords. Trolls, while not having particularly scientific minds, long ago figured this much out.

So there we were, Troll and I, he dining on M. de Gruff's billy goats, large and small and in-between. And after each meal, after he had a round of belching and farting—which trolls consider good form—he favored me with a troll tale.

He told me about trolls in love and trolls at war—which to the untutored ear can sound much the same.

He told me a tale about a troll who lived in the waters near Nôtre-Dame, eating fish and fishermen. But that troll conceived an unlikely passion for the cathedral. He desired to talk to the gargoyles, whom he thought must be cousins of his. He began to waste away with longing for just a single word with his stone kin. So he pulled himself up out of the water and started across the land. After three steps he died, of course. The Parisians used his bones for soup and built a monument where he fell. But he died happy—or so Troll said.

He told me about a troll who had been interviewed by a journalist, and when I asked what paper the piece had appeared in, he giggled, an unlikely sound coming from such a large source. The silly troll, he said, had eaten the man *before* he wrote the story, not after. We had a good laugh about that!

And then he told me about his mother, about the good times before his father had given him a shove. We cried together. After all, that's what friends are for.

He was so delighted with my company, he tried to compose a troll song to the beauty of my span, but he got lost in rhymes about tans/fans/bans and never did finish it. But he was a good teller of tales.

And I am the consummate listener.

I must admit that—except for the day Mme. d'Aulnoy and Mme. le Prince du Beaumont traded stories sitting on the banks of my stream, their *petit* picnic spread out on a blanket—I was never happier.

But the sad fact is that trolls are not very smart. Good storytellers, yes. Pleasant companions, quite. Undemanding friends, absolutely. But they lack upstairs what they have elsewhere. Breadth. They are—alas— really quite stupid. They do not have the slightest understanding of diplomatic dissembling. They do not know how to prevaricate—or to put it more succinctly, they cannot tell a lie. Even with my coaching, Troll would not move downstream a ways and take goats from different parts of the river just to fool them.

"I like it here with you," he said. "Besides, this is my place."

And not being a troll myself, I couldn't shove him off.

So the day came when the goats stopped crossing the bridge because it had become too notably dangerous. For a month not a single one went over my span. And while I was delighted to be rid of that constant, demned trit-trot, trit-trot, it worried me to see my friend grow so thin and wan. It got so one could almost read a book through him. He had not even the energy to tell stories.

So I did what I could. Bridges are not a flighty tribe. We are solid and stolid. We stay put. But we have our wiles for all that. One does not arch over a river for so many years without learning something.

I waited until one rather silly young goat strayed a bit too close to my embankments and I called to him.

"Come here, little goat."

He looked about cautiously. "Are you a troll?"

"A troll? Do I look like a troll?"

"Well, actually you look like a bridge."

"And have you ever *seen* a troll?"

He shook his little nubbined head.

"But you *have* seen a bridge?"

He giggled. I knew then that I had him.

"So if you have never seen a troll, how do you know they exist?"

"My mother warned me about them."

I allowed myself a deprecating little laugh. "Mothers! I bet she also warned you about eating tins and paper products and staying out too late at night."

He nodded.

"I am just a bridge," I said. "Immobile and proper. And of course, on my other side is..."

"A green meadow?" he asked.

"Greener than any you have ever seen," I said.

That did it. He upped and started over. Trit-trot, trit-trot.

Of course, halfway there, Troll came up and grabbed the fool off and had his first good dinner in a month. Well, *good* dinner is perhaps an exaggeration. It was only a very little goat. Practically a kid.

If only he had been content with the one. But the next goat I snared for him with my promise of greener pastures was middle sized.

"Let this one go over," I whispered to Troll, "and you will soon have the entire herd wanting to follow." Even though I mentally cringed at the idea of so many *trits* and so many *trots*, I did not want my friend to die.

But that smacked too much of planning, something trolls have no sense about. And lying, which they know nothing of at all.

"Hungry *now!*" Troll complained, and ate the middle-sized de Gruff goat right then and there.

So when the big goat followed, with horns as

sharp as gaffing hooks and a sly twist of mind, it is no wonder that my dear Troll was taken in.

It was not the fall that killed him, of course. It was when the big billy goat of M. de Gruff lifted him out of the water. Troll was dead long before he hit the ground.

My own fault then, you will say, that I must endure this trit-trot, trit-trot all day long. I do not, myself, accept blame. Life is like a river: forever changing. Sometimes it is at flood stage, and sometimes not.

But if you should hear of another troll who is looking for a home, tell him there is a Bridge of Slight Consequence placed between two green meadows not far from Avignon. Fish abound in the water, and goats gambol on the hills. And if he is not too greedy a troll, he can make a good living here. Besides, he will have an excellent listener to his tales. What troll could resist that?

Brandon and the Aliens

BRANDON SAW THE FIRST ALIEN on Monday, and he stopped for a quick look, but he didn't tell a soul what he saw. Not at first. He didn't think anyone would believe him. He hardly believed it himself.

He had been bicycling home from Freddy's house and he was late as usual, so he didn't mean to stop at all. But when he caught a glimpse of the alien squatting partway behind a rhododendron bush next to the bike path, he had to look. Who wouldn't?

The alien was gray and rubber-legged, without a visible mouth, and about five feet tall, which was taller than Freddy. It was eating a live robin. Eating it, but not in any ordinary way. And there were these strange juices—as gray as the alien but lumpy, like an old moldy stew someone had forgotten to clean out of the pot—sloshing around its feet. It was pretty disgusting, even to Brandon, and he was the one in his family who liked the movies with the grossest special effects.

He could smell the alien from where he was, and it didn't make him want to get any closer. Like burnt eggs combined with unwashed hockey socks. He blinked—and the alien was gone. All it left behind were a few robin feathers—and that smell.

Brandon saw the second alien on Tuesday, and he didn't tell about that one, either, even though this one was green and was finishing off a squirrel. Brandon figured no one would actually believe him about the aliens, anyway. He had a reputation, after all, and it wasn't exactly for telling the truth. His father said he stretched things too often and his mother said he had only a nodding acquaintance with reality. His teacher had once called him a name that rhymed with "fire," and not in a joking way, either.

On Wednesday he saw the third alien—a red one—eating a raccoon. By then it was really too late to tell because by Wednesday, *everyone* knew about them. And the aliens were moving up and down the food chain faster than anyone could imagine, eating all kinds of animals, from birds to squirrels to rabbits to raccoons to cats and dogs.

The way everyone got to know about the aliens was that Old Lady Montague's barn cats disappeared in an awful gray slosh while she watched from her kitchen window. She dialed 911 immediately, plaguing the police with stories about three Martians landing. Of course, she'd done that before, so they didn't really believe her right away. But then Colonel Brighton's pit bull, the one that had bitten three kids and had to wear a muzzle, was slurped up while the colonel and a neighbor looked on. So this time the police *had* to listen. However, by the time the police arrived, all that was left of the dog were a couple of toenails, its heavy chain, the muzzle, and that awful smell.

Hard Copy sent a reporter to cover the invasion, if you can call three aliens an invasion; which of course the reporter did, though only those three—the gray, the green, and the red—were ever seen. Brandon's science teacher was interviewed, and Captain Covey of the state police was, too. Even the mayor said a few words, because it was an election year, though he was cut off in midsentence by a commercial. But really, all they managed was "We haven't a clue." A conservative study group blamed satanists, the D&D after-school gaming society, and proponents of the ERA, in that order. Everybody was hoping for Oprah or Rikki Lake, and one group of mothers from a nursery play group actually put a call in to Montel. All they got was *Hard Copy*. *Hard Copy* had no pictures, except of the townspeople talking, because the three creatures didn't seem to stay in any one place long enough, unless you counted the smell they left behind. No one could figure out where they'd be next, and you can't videotape an odor.

"The reporter should have interviewed me. I could have told him plenty," Brandon complained to Freddy over the phone. "After all, I saw the aliens first, up close and personal. When they were still working on just the small stuff." But Freddy was mad at him for not having said anything on Monday, so Freddy wasn't quite as sympathetic as he could have been.

Brandon knew the grown-ups were really getting scared when Dad drove him and his sister to school, then picked them up after school and drove them home again. He showed them how to use the pellet gun, the fire extinguisher, and the pepper spray. Mom canceled their piano lessons, Brandon's hockey practice, Kathy's ballet class, and the paper. Well, she didn't exactly cancel the paper. But the paperboy refused to deliver any more.

In effect, the entire family was grounded.

Heck—the entire town was grounded.

"And all just because of three hungry aliens," Brandon complained to Freddy's answering machine. Freddy and his family weren't answering in person. They had gone for a long visit to Freddy's grandmother, who lived in Miami. They weren't coming back till the aliens were gone. "At least Miami's aliens are human," the machine said with Freddy's stepdad's voice.

By now the aliens had moved on to horses. And cows. CNN came to town and reported that, so it had to be true. But no one knew why the aliens were there, except as a bold new venture in eating out. Going where no aliens had gone before. That kind of stuff. And no one had gotten close enough yet to deal with them directly, since they just ate and ran, leaving behind only their signature odor as a kind of calling card.

So the sheriff suggested everyone in town move into shelters until the invasion was over. "Until they move to Greener Pastures," is what Sheriff Cooper actually said. Greener Pastures was a town in the next county. It was an old joke, only nobody was laughing.

No one could figure out how the aliens went from one place to another, either. For example, one minute they would all be at the town dump, digesting seagulls; the next in the backyard of Dr. Foster's kennels, munching on guinea pigs and poodles. Each time the state police arrived, the aliens were already gone somewhere else, eating their way through a herd of Holsteins or an entire Morgan horse farm. In a rural county like ours, the police couldn't possibly stake out all of the animals. And everyone who had been near the aliens was too frightened to describe them accurately, except for the smell. And of course now that they had been seen, everyone knew they were aliens. The sheriff called for the National Guard.

One farmer had tried unloading a shotgun into the green alien from about thirty paces when it ate his goat herd. The shot bounced off the alien's body, but the farmer got the alien's attention, all right, which was not exactly what he was going for. When the Guard got there, he was in his car, the doors locked tight, babbling into his CB radio, calling for a stealth bomber and otherwise making no sense whatever. There was an odd slime on the outside door handle of the car and the burnt egg–hockey socks smell was everywhere. Five biologists came from Atlanta and said the slime was probably some kind of stomach acid, though they would have to do some tests to be certain. They set up a lab at the university. Of course no one was sure the aliens even had stomachs "as we know them," some ET specialist said. The aliens sure didn't have discernible mouths. Or at least they didn't have mouths where mouths were supposed to be; this much Brandon knew.

But still no one could predict where the aliens were going to be, only report where they had been. They jaunted from animal to animal like kids at a wedding buffet. Even the scientists were baffled.

Brandon had an idea, though, about where the aliens might be found, though his father absolutely refused to believe him or let him call the authorities. When Brandon suggested that having seen the aliens three separate times, he was the town expert on them, his dad gave him the Look. The Look usually preceded the Lecture on "Making Things Up" which is what his father said instead of the other l-word.

Brandon backed down at once. After the Look and the Lecture, he was usually sent to bed early. *That* was not part of his plan.

But now Brandon knew that he would have to go it alone, without any grown-up help.

"Me, too," Kathy pleaded.

"You're only eight," Brandon answered. "I'm eleven."

"Not till Thursday," Kathy said.

That settled it, of course. There's nothing like a kid sister to make a boy do something he has hoped to be talked out of.

"By then the aliens will be long gone," Brandon promised her. And he meant it. Or at least he *hoped* he meant it.

"At least tell me where the aliens are going to be," Kathy begged.

"On the bike path," Brandon said at last. He had to tell someone, and Freddy was still in Miami.

"Why the bike path?" Kathy asked.

"Because it's the only place in town they've been spotted three separate times."

"So?" Little sisters can be a hard sell.

"Maybe that's where the Mother Ship is."

"What's a Mother Ship?"

He sighed. "The place where all those mothers come from," he said in a grumbling voice.

"How do you know they're mothers? Maybe one of them is a father. Or a baby."

He turned away. "I'm going to kill Freddy for leaving," he muttered as he pulled on his goalie's gear. As usual, the shin pads gave him a moment's worth of trouble. Then he straightened up and got into the rest. If any aliens tried to eat him, they'd need some pretty strong teeth. He tapped the face mask with his gloves. Riding his bike was going to be hard, especially wearing a cup and skates. And it was hard seeing to the side with the mask. But his gear was almost as good as a suit of armor—and about as expensive! He'd taken many a blade to the shin in practice and in games and hardly felt a thing. Just a bit of bruising. He doubted any alien could eat him through all that leather and plastic. After all, they had not eaten the muzzle, the dogs' tags, the horses' halters, or the reins.

"Shouldn't you ask Dad if you can go out? Especially in your gear?" Kathy asked.

"Don't..." Brandon said, going over to her and thumping the top of her head with his glove, "even think about telling anyone what I am doing."

"Not even Mom?"

"Especially not Mom," he said.

"Why?"

"Because...well, because she'll faint."

"I've never seen her faint. Not even when I cut my finger and there was blood everywhere and Dad had to sit down."

"Well, you'll see her faint if you tell her about this. It's a secret. Between you and me."

"Like the secrets you have with Freddy?" she asked.

"Only better."

She smiled. "Only better," she said.

By this he knew she would never tell. She had always been jealous of his secrets with Freddy, which was just as it should be. She was three years younger than he was, after all. He and Freddy were eleven. Almost.

Actually, riding the bike wasn't as difficult as Brandon had feared. The hockey stick across the handlebars was awkward, but he could manage it. He couldn't go very fast, but he wasn't in that much of a hurry. In fact, the farther along he got, the slower he went, and that had nothing to do with either the hockey stick or the skates. To be honest—and though he wasn't always truthful with his parents or his sister or his teacher, he was always honest with himself— he was scared.

Not a little scared.

A lot scared.

After all, these aliens were eating horses! And cows! And they had polished off Colonel Brighton's awful pit bull without so much as a burp. Of course, it had been muzzled. But still...

With each street, Brandon's stomach shrank with terror, until by the time he got to the bike path that led to Freddy's house, there was nothing left in his belly but a small hard rock. Still he pedaled on. He was afraid of the aliens but he was even more afraid that if he turned back now Kathy would tell all her friends at Hawley Elementary that he was scared. So even if he were alive at the end of this, he might as well be dead, with eight-year-old girls laughing at him.

He was debating this with himself when he turned onto the bike path, and there, squatting over the remains of a rabbit, as if it had just been snacking or having dessert, was one of the aliens.

The gray one.

This time Brandon didn't look at it from the corner of his eye or through a rhododendron bush. He looked at it full on.

It really *was* gross.

Well, *gross* didn't half explain it. The alien had shiny, slick dark gray skin, as if it were constantly wet. Its head—if that *was* a head—was bulbous, like a giant onion, and it bulged in funny, awkward places. Its eyes were twin black shrouds without pupils. It had slimy tentacles that flopped about. In fact, Brandon suddenly knew *exactly* what the alien looked like.

"A big gray jellyfish!" he said aloud. Right—a jellyfish with a shark's skin.

The alien didn't seem to notice him. It kept slurping up the rabbit.

Until, that is, Brandon dropped his hockey stick and the stick kind of shimmied on the pavement, making a lot of noise.

Then the gray alien noticed him big-time!

It seemed to hunch down on itself, then lifted up with a kind of long sucking sound—a sort of sssssssssssssluuuurrrrrrppppp. It landed on the hockey stick and stayed there for a moment before deciding that the stick was inedible. Then it turned its black-shroud eyes on Brandon.

Brandon was so frightened he couldn't move. Which probably saved him for the moment. Clearly the alien only ate living things. And living things moved. Brandon wasn't moving. He was too scared to.

Suddenly there was a sound behind him and a little voice called out, "Brandon, where are you?"

He turned his head slowly, cautiously, and looked through the mask's slit.

That was when Kathy's bike came into view.

The alien turned its head, too. Then it turned its body and, as if swimming through both air and time, it focused on her.

"Oh," Kathy said in a voice that was little and frightened. "Oh."

"Don't move!" Brandon cried out. "Don't move a muscle, Kathy." But his voice was straining through the mask and Kathy was clearly too far gone with fright to hear him anyway. She braked the bike and tried to turn to go back the way she had come. But the bike wobbled left, then right, then fell over with Kathy still on it. At that, the alien hunched down on itself and then began to lift up.

That's when Brandon lost it. No one—alien or not—messed with his little sister. He got off the bike, reached down, picked up the hockey stick, straightened up, and charged.

Of course it was a bit awkward, because he was wearing skates and there wasn't any ice around, it being the middle of August. He was sweating like stink from fear and from the heat. Perspiration ran down his face, making him almost blind behind the mask. And he was still holding his bike. Whatever heroics he had planned turned at that moment into pure disaster. He tripped over something in the bike path and fell onto the alien, hockey stick flailing.

"Oof," he said. And "Jeeze." And "Unh-unh." His hockey coach would have benched him for that kind of move.

The alien completely forgot about Kathy, though. It raised up a bit, made its slurping noise, which—close up—sounded like the whirring of a giant Mixmaster, only worse. There was a sudden sharp spray, like soapy water, that further obscured Brandon's vision, and then the alien landed on him, sliding down him like a kid on a banister, from his head to his feet, totally encasing him in a wet dark that smelled a little like second-day underwear, more like the boys' locker room after a game, and a lot like a whole pot of burnt eggs.

For a moment Brandon was totally without feeling or thought. And then he realized that he was about to die. About to die—and there was nothing he could do to change things. Or to say good-bye. It was going to be messy, ugly, and embarrassing. He was closed up inside the alien—an alien that had already devoured birds, squirrels, raccoons, dogs, cats, even horses and cows.

Then the alien's entire body shuddered, convulsed, and...lifted off, flopping away from him. Brandon realized that he was alive and out in the summer sun again, smelling like throw-up and feeling worse.

He couldn't see much, for the mask had slipped a bit sideways and he was covered with a variety of substances, none of which he wanted to put a name to. But someone—*Kathy?*—was shouting his name.

He turned. He tried to listen. Then he remembered.

"Kathy!" he cried. "Get away. Go home. The alien..."

He heard a lot of other sounds then. Someone took his mask off. Someone wiped his face. When he opened his eyes to the summer sun, there were his mom and his dad and the fire chief and Captain Covey and Brandon's science teacher. And the CNN reporter was standing on the side, his microphone at the ready, looking happy.

On the ground was the gray alien, covered with a soapy foam and looking very very dead.

"I don't...get it..." Brandon started to say, when the reporter moved in.

"What does it feel like, being the brother of a hero?" the reporter asked, shoving the mike under his nose.

The two words didn't connect: brother...hero.

"He feels fine," his mom said.

"We all feel fine," his dad said.

Kathy was crying. "I had to come," she was blubbing, "because I left Mom a note that I had seen the aliens on the bike path and was going there." She snuffled loudly. " 'Cause I promised I wouldn't say you were going, and besides, she'd never have believed you. And she must have told Dad. And he called the police and..."

And then Brandon noticed what Kathy was holding in her hand: a fire extinguisher. The one from behind the kitchen door. The yellow one that Dad had had them practice with. There was something still dribbling out of the nozzle. Foam. He looked down at his feet, where his skates were covered in the same foam. And covered with something else as well. He didn't want to know what the something else was.

The sheriff lured the CNN reporter away from Brandon by talking into his microphone. "Like when my mama used to wash my mouth out with soap for saying naughty words," he told forty million viewers. "That alien didn't like it any more than I did all those years ago. *Ptooie!*" He laughed. He had his arm around the reporter, who was looking around for help. "We'll do the same with them other two. Wash their mouths out with soap."

"More like an enema," Brandon's mom said.

"Myrna!" his dad said, but he was laughing.

Which is how Brandon knew there was nothing more to worry about. Not even ruining his hockey gear, which cost $398 new. Nothing at all.

Except—he suddenly thought with growing horror as the TV cameras continued to roll—all the kids at school who would laugh and laugh at him because he'd been rescued by an eight-year-old. He knew then, with absolute certainty, that it would have been better if he *had* been eaten by an alien, the gray or the green or the red.

Much better. All things considered.

Winter's King

HE WAS NOT BORN a king but the child of wandering players, slipping out ice-blue in the deepest part of winter, when the wind howled outside the little green caravan. The midwife pronounced him dead, her voice smoothly hiding her satisfaction. She had not wanted to be called to a birth on such a night.

But the father, who sang for pennies and smiles from strangers, grabbed the child from her and plunged him into a basin of lukewarm water, all the while singing a strange fierce song in a tongue he did not really know.

Slowly the child turned pink in the water, as if breath were lent him by both the water and the song. He coughed once and spit up a bit of rosy blood, then wailed a note that was a minor third higher than his father's last surprised tone.

Without taking time to swaddle the child, the

father laid him dripping wet and kicking next to his wife on the caravan bed. As she lifted the babe to her breast, the woman smiled at her husband, a look that included both the man and the child but cut the midwife cold.

The old woman muttered something that was part curse, part fear, then more loudly said, "No good will come of this dead cold child. He shall thrive in winter but never in the warm and he shall think little of this world. I have heard of such before. They are called Winter's Kin."

The mother sat up in bed, careful not to disturb the child at her side. "Then he shall be a Winter King, more than any of his kin or kind," she said. "But worry not, old woman, you shall be paid for the live child, as well as the dead." She nodded to her husband, who paid the midwife twice over from his meager pocket, six copper coins.

The midwife made the sign of horns over the money, but still she kept it and, wrapping her cloak tightly around her stout body and a scarf around her head, she walked out into the storm. Not twenty steps from the caravan, the wind tore the cloak from her and pulled tight the scarf about her neck. An icy branch broke from a tree and smashed in the side of her head. In the morning when she was found, she was frozen solid. The money she had clutched in her hand was gone.

The player was hanged for the murder and his

wife left to mourn, even as she nursed the child. Then she married quickly, for the shelter and the food. Her new man never liked the winter babe.

"He is a cold one," the husband said. "He hears voices in the wind," though it was he who was cold and who, when filled with drink, heard the dark counsel of unnamed gods who told him to beat his wife and abuse her son. The woman never complained, for she feared for her child. Yet strangely the child did not seem to care. He paid more attention to the sounds of the wind than the shouts of his stepfather, lending his own voice to the cries he alone could hear, though always a minor third above.

As the midwife had prophesied, in winter he was an active child, his eyes bright and quick to laugh. But once spring came, the buds in his cheeks faded, even as the ones on the boughs grew big. In the summer and well into the fall, he was animated only when his mother told him tales of Winter's Kin, and though she made up the tales as only a player can, he knew the stories all to be true.

When the winter child was ten, his mother died of her brutal estate and the boy left into the howl of a storm, without either cloak or hat between him and the cold. Drunk, his ten-year father did not see him go. The boy did not go to escape the man's beatings; he went to his kin, who called him from the wind. Barefooted and bareheaded, he crossed the snows trying to catch up with the riders in the storm. He saw them clearly. They were clad in great white capes, the hoods lined with ermine; and when they turned to look at him, their eyes were wind blue and the bones of their faces were thin and fine.

Long, long he trailed behind them, his tears turned to ice. He wept not for his dead mother, for it was she who had tied him to the world. He wept for himself and his feet, which were too small to follow after the fast-riding Winter's Kin.

A woodcutter found him that night and dragged him home, plunging him into a bath of lukewarm water and speaking in a strange tongue that even he, in all his wanderings, had never heard.

The boy turned pink in the water, as if life had been returned to him by both the bathing and the prayer, but he did not thank the old man when he woke. Instead he turned his face to the window and wept, this time like any child, the tears falling like soft rain down his cheeks.

"Why do you weep?" the old man asked.

"For my mother and for the wind," the boy said. "And for what I cannot have."

The winter child stayed five years with the old woodcutter, going out each day with him to haul the kindling home. They always went into the woods to the south, a scraggly, ungraceful copse of second-growth trees, but never to the woods to the north.

"That is the great Ban Forest," the old man said. "All that lies therein belongs to the king."

"The king," the boy said, remembering his mother's tales. "And so I am."

"And so are we all in God's heaven," the old man said. "But here on earth I am a woodcutter and you are a foundling boy. The wood to the south be ours."

Though the boy paid attention to what the old man said in the spring and summer and fall, once winter arrived he heard only the voices in the wind. Often the old man would find him standing nearly naked by the door and have to lead him back to the fire, where the boy would sink down in a stupor and say nothing at all.

The old man tried to make light of such times, and would tell the boy tales while he warmed at the hearth. He told him of Mother Holle and her feather bed, of Godfather Death, and of the Singing Bone. He told him of the Flail of Heaven and the priest whose rod sprouted flowers because the Water Nix had a soul. But the boy had ears only for the voices in the wind, and what stories he heard there, he did not tell.

The old man died at the tag end of their fifth winter, and the boy left without even folding the hands of the corpse. He walked into the southern copse, for that was the way his feet knew. But the Winter Kin were not about.

The winds were gentle here, and spring had already softened the bitter brown branches to a muted rose. A yellow-green haze haloed the air and underfoot the muddy soil smelled moist and green and new.

The boy slumped to the ground and wept, not for the death of the woodcutter, nor for his mother's death, but for the loss once more of his kin. He knew it would be a long time till winter came again.

And then, from far away, he heard a final wild burst of music. A stray strand of cold wind snapped under his nose, as strong as a smelling bottle. His eyes opened wide and, without thinking, he stood.

Following the trail of song, as clear to him as cobbles on a city street, he moved toward the great Ban Forest, where the heavy trees still shadowed over winter storms. Crossing the fresh new furze between the woods, he entered the old dark forest and wound around the tall, black trees, in and out of shadows, going as true north as a needle in a water-filled bowl. The path grew cold and the once-muddy ground gave way to frost.

At first all he saw was a mist, as white as if the hooves of horses had struck up dust from sheer ice. But when he blinked once and then twice, he saw coming toward him a great company of fair folk, some on steeds the color of clouds and some on steeds the color of snow. And he realized all at once that it was no mist he had seen, but the breath of those great white stallions.

"My people," he cried at last. "My kin. My kind."
And he tore off first his boots, then his trousers, and
at last his shirt, until he was free of the world and
its possessions and could run toward the Winter Kin
naked and unafraid.

On the first horse was a woman of unearthly
beauty. Her hair was plaited in a hundred white
braids and on her head was a crown of diamonds and
moonstones. Her eyes were wind blue and there was
frost in her breath. Slowly she dismounted and com-
manded the stallion to be still. Then she took an ermine cape from across the saddle, holding it open to
receive the boy.

"My king," she sang, "my own true love," and
swaddled him in the cloud white cloak.

He answered her, his voice a minor third lower
than hers. "My queen, my own true love. I am come
home."

When the king's foresters caught up to him, the
feathered arrow was fast in his breast, but there was,
surprisingly, no blood. He was lying, arms out-
stretched, like an angel in the snow.

"He was just a wild boy, just that lackwit, the one
who brought home kindling with the old man," said
one.

"Nevertheless, he was in the king's forest," said
the other. "He knew better than that."

"Naked as a newborn," said the first. "But look!"

In the boy's left hand were three copper coins, three more in his right.

"Twice the number needed for the birthing of a babe," said the first forester.

"Just enough," said his companion, "to buy a wooden casket and a man to dig the grave."

And they carried the cold body out of the wood, heeding neither the music nor the voices singing wild and strange hosannas in the wind.

Lost Girls

I T ISN'T FAIR!" Darla complained to her mom for the third time during their bedtime reading. She meant it wasn't fair that Wendy only did the housework in Neverland and that Peter Pan and the boys got to fight Captain Hook.

"Well, I can't change it," Mom said in her even, lawyer voice. "That's just the way it is in the book. Your argument is with Mr. Barrie, the author, and he's long dead. Should I go on?"

"Yes. No. I don't know," Darla said, coming down on both sides of the question, as she often did.

Mom shrugged and closed the book, and *that* was the end of the night's reading.

Darla watched impassively as her mom got up and left the room, snapping off the bedside lamp as she went. When she closed the door there was just a rim of light from the hall showing around three sides of the door, making it look like something out of a science fiction movie. Darla pulled the covers up over her nose. Her breath made the space feel like a little oven.

"Not fair at all," Darla said to the dark, and she didn't just mean the book. She wasn't the least bit sleepy.

But the house made its comfortable night-settling noises around her: the breathy whispers of the hot air through the vents, the ticking of the grandfather clock in the hall, the sound of the maple branch scritch-scratching against the clapboard siding. They were a familiar lullaby, comforting and soothing. Darla didn't mean to go to sleep, but she did.

Either that or she stepped out of her bed and walked through the closed door into Neverland.

Take your pick.

It didn't feel at all like a dream to Darla. The details were too exact. And she could smell things. She'd never smelled anything in a dream before. So Darla had no reason to believe that what happened to her next was anything but real.

One minute she had gotten up out of bed, heading for the bathroom, and the very next she was sliding down the trunk of a very large, smooth tree. The trunk was unlike any of the maples in her yard, being a kind of yellowish color. It felt almost slippery under her hands and smelled like bananas gone slightly bad. Her nightgown made a sound like whooosh as she slid along.

When she landed on the ground, she tripped over a large root and stubbed her toe.

"Ow!" she said.

"Shhh!" cautioned someone near her.

She looked up and saw two boys in matching ragged cutoffs and T-shirts staring at her. "Shhh! yourselves," she said, wondering at the same time who they were.

But it hadn't been those boys who spoke. A third boy, behind her, tapped her on the shoulder and whispered, "If you aren't quiet, *He* will find us."

She turned, ready to ask who *He* was. But the boy, dressed in green tights and a green shirt and a rather silly green hat, and smelling like fresh lavender, held a finger up to his lips. They were perfect lips. Like a movie star's. Darla knew him at once.

"Peter," she whispered. "Peter Pan."

He swept the hat off and gave her a deep bow. "Wendy," he countered.

"Well, Darla, actually," she said.

"Wendy Darla," he said. "Give us a thimble."

She and her mom had read that part in the book already, where Peter got kiss and thimble mixed up, and she guessed what it was he really meant, but she wasn't about to kiss him. She was much too young to be kissing boys. Especially boys she'd just met. And he had to be more a man than a boy, anyway, no matter how young he looked. The copy of *Peter Pan* she and her mother had been reading had belonged to her grandmother originally. Besides, Darla wasn't sure she liked Peter. Of couse, she wasn't sure she didn't like him. It was a bit confusing. Darla hated

things being confusing, like her parents' divorce and
her dad's new young wife and their twins who
were—and who weren't exactly—her brothers.

"I don't have a thimble," she said, pretending not
to understand.

"I have," he said, smiling with persuasive boyish
charm. "Can I give it to you?"

But she looked down at her feet in order not to
answer, which was how she mostly responded to her
dad these days, and that was that. At least for the
moment. She didn't want to think any further ahead,
and neither, it seemed, did Peter.

He shrugged and took her hand, dragging her
down a path that smelled of moldy old leaves. Darla
was too surprised to protest. And besides, Peter was
lots stronger than she was. The two boys followed.
When they got to a large dark brown tree whose
odor reminded Darla of her grandmother's wardrobe,
musty and ancient, Peter stopped. He let go of her
hand and jumped up on one of the twisted roots that
were looped over and around one another like woody
snakes. Darla was suddenly reminded of her school
principal when he towered above the students at as-
sembly. He was a tall man but the dais he stood on
made him seem even taller. When you sat in the front
row, you could look up his nose. She could look up
Peter's nose now. Like her principal, he didn't look
so grand that way. Or so threatening.

"Here's where we live," Peter said, his hand in a
large sweeping motion. Throwing his head back, he

crowed like a rooster; he no longer seemed afraid of making noise. Then he said, "You'll like it."

"Maybe I will. Maybe I won't," Darla answered, talking to her feet again.

Peter's perfect mouth made a small pout as if that weren't the response he'd been expecting. Then he jumped down into a dark space between the roots. The other boys followed him. Not to be left behind, in case that rooster crow really had called something awful to them, Darla went after the boys into the dark place. She found what they had actually gone through was a door that was still slightly ajar.

The door opened on to a long, even darker passage that wound into the very center of the tree; the passage smelled damp, like bathing suits left still wet in a closet. Peter and the boys seemed to know the way without any need of light. But Darla was constantly afraid of stumbling and she was glad when someone reached out and held her hand.

Then one last turn and there was suddenly plenty of light from hundreds of little candles set in holders that were screwed right into the living heart of the wood. By the candlelight she saw it was Peter who had hold of her hand.

"Welcome to Neverland," Peter said, as if this were supposed to be a big surprise.

Darla took her hand away from his. "It's smaller than I thought it would be," she said. This time she looked right at him.

Peter's perfect mouth turned down again. "It's big

enough for us," he said. Then as if a sudden thought had struck him, he smiled. "But too small for *Him*." He put his back to Darla and shouted, "Let's have a party. We've got us a new Wendy."

Suddenly, from all corners of the room, boys came tumbling and stumbling and dancing, and pushing one another to get a look at her. They were shockingly noisy and all smelled like unwashed socks. One of them made fart noises with his mouth. She wondered if any of them had taken a bath recently. They were worse—Darla thought—than her Stemple cousins, who were so awful their parents never took them anywhere anymore, not out to a restaurant or the movies or anyplace at all.

"Stop it!" she said.

The boys stopped at once.

"I told you," Peter said. "She's a regular Wendy, all right. She's even given me a thimble."

Darla's jaw dropped at the lie. *How could he?*

She started to say "I did not!" but the boys were already cheering so loudly her protestations went unheard.

"Tink," Peter called, and one of the candles detached itself from the heartwood to flutter around his head, "tell the Wendys we want a Welcome Feast."

The Wendys? Darla bit her lip. *What did Peter mean by that?*

The little light flickered on and off. *A kind of code,*

Darla thought. She assumed it was the fairy Tinker Bell, but she couldn't really make out what this Tink looked like except for that flickering, fluttering presence. But as if understanding Peter's request, the flicker took off toward a black corner and, shedding but a little light, flew right into the dark.

"Good old Tink," Peter said, and he smiled at Darla with such practice, dimples appeared simultaneously on both sides of his mouth.

"What kind of food..." Darla began.

"Everything parents won't let you have," Peter answered. "Sticky buns and tipsy cake and Butterfingers and brownies and..."

The boys gathered around them, chanting the names as if they were the lyrics to some kind of song, adding, "...apple tarts and gingerbread and chocolate mousse and trifle and..."

"And stomachaches and sugar highs," Darla said stubbornly. "My dad's a nutritionist. I'm only allowed healthy food."

Peter turned his practiced dimpled smile on her again. "Forget your father. You're in Neverland now, and no one need ever go back home from here."

At that Darla burst into tears, half in frustration and half in fear. She actually liked her dad, as well as loved him, despite the fact that he'd left her for his new wife, and despite the fact of the twins, who were actually adorable as long as she didn't have to live with them. The thought that she'd been caught in Neverland with no way to return was so awful, she couldn't help crying.

Peter shrugged and turned to the boys. "Girls!" he said with real disgust.

"All Wendys!" they shouted back at him.

Darla wiped her eyes, and spoke right to Peter. "My name is *not* Wendy," she said clearly. "It's Darla."

Peter looked at her, and there was nothing nice or laughing or young about his eyes. They were dark and cold and very very old.

Darla shivered.

"*Here* you're a Wendy," he said.

And with that, the dark place where Tink had disappeared grew increasingly light, as a door opened and fifteen girls carrying trays piled high with cakes, cookies, biscuits, buns, and other kinds of goodies marched single file into the hall. They were led by a tall, slender, pretty girl with brown hair that fell straight to her shoulders.

The room suddenly smelled overpoweringly of that sickly sweetness of children's birthday parties at school, when their mothers brought in sloppy cupcakes greasy with icing. Darla shuddered.

"Welcome Feast!" shouted the boy who was closest to the door. He made a deep bow.

"Welcome Feast!" they all shouted, laughing and gathering around a great center table.

Only Darla seemed to notice that not one of the Wendys was smiling.

The Feast went on for ages, because each of the boys had to stand up and give a little speech. Of course, most of them only said, "Welcome, Wendy!" and "Glad to meet you!" before sitting down again. A few elaborated a little bit more. But Peter more than made up for it with a long, rambling talk about duty and dessert and how no one loved them out in the World Above as much as he did here in Neverland, and how the cakes proved that.

The boys cheered and clapped at each of Peter's pronouncements, and threw buns and scones across the table at one another as a kind of punctuation. Tink circled Peter's head continuously like a crown of stars, though she never really settled.

But the girls, standing behind the boys like banquet waitresses, did not applaud. Rather they shifted from foot to foot, looking alternately apprehensive and bored. One, no more than four years old, kept yawning behind a chubby hand.

After a polite bite of an apple tart, which she couldn't swallow but spit into her napkin, Darla didn't even try to pretend. The little pie had been much too sweet, not tart at all. And even though Peter kept urging her between the welcomes to eat something, she just couldn't. That small rebellion seemed to annoy him enormously and he stood up once again, this time on the tabletop, to rant on about how some people lacked gratitude, and how difficult it was to provide for so many, especially with Him about.

Peter never actually looked at Darla as he spoke, but she knew—and everyone else knew—that he meant *she* was the ungrateful one. That bothered her some, but not as much as it might have. She even found herself enjoying the fact that he was annoyed, and that realization almost made her smile.

When Peter ended with "No more Feasts for them with Bad Attitudes!" the boys leaped from their benches and overturned the big table, mashing the remaining food into the floor. Then they all disappeared, diving down a variety of bolt-holes, with Tink after them, leaving the girls alone in the big candlelit room.

"Now see what you've done," said the oldest girl, the pretty one with the straight brown hair. Obviously the leader of the Wendys, she wore a simple dark dress—*like a uniform*, Darla thought, *a school uniform that's badly stained*. "It's going to take forever to get that stuff off the floor. Ages and ages. Mops and buckets. And nothing left for us to eat."

The other girls agreed loudly.

"*They* made the mess," Darla said sensibly. "Let *them* clean it up! That's how it's done at my house."

There was a horrified silence. For a long moment none of the girls said a word, but their mouths opened and shut like fish on beaches. Finally the littlest one spoke.

"Peter won't 'ike it."

"Well, I don't 'ike Peter!" Darla answered quickly. "He's nothing but a long-winded bully."

"But," said the little Wendy, "you gave him a thimble." She actually said "simble."

"No," Darla said. "Peter lied. I didn't."

The girls all seemed dumbstruck by that revelation. Without a word more, they began to clean the room, first righting the table and then laboriously picking up what they could with their fingers before resorting, at last, to the dreaded buckets and mops. Soon the place smelled like any institution after a cleaning, like a school bathroom or a hospital corridor, Lysol-fresh with an overcast of pine.

Shaking her head, Darla just watched them until the littlest Wendy handed her a mop.

Darla flung the mop to the floor. "I won't do it," she said. "It's not fair."

The oldest Wendy came over to her and put her hand on Darla's shoulder. "Who ever told you that life is fair?" she asked. "Certainly not a navvy, nor an upstairs maid, nor a poor man trying to feed his family."

"Nor my da," put in one of the girls. She was pale skinned, sharp nosed, gap toothed, homely to a fault. "He allas said life was a crapshoot and all usn's got was snake-eyes."

"And not my father," said another, a whey-faced, doughy-looking eight-year-old. "He used to always say that the world didn't treat him right."

"What I mean is that it's not fair that they get to have the adventures and you get to clean the house," Darla explained carefully.

"Who will clean it if we don't?" Wendy asked. She picked up the mop and handed it back to Darla. "Not them. Not ever. So if we want it done, we do it. Fair is not the matter here." She went back to her place in the line of girls mopping the floor.

With a sigh that was less a capitulation and more a show of solidarity with the Wendys, Darla picked up her own mop and followed.

When the room was set to rights again, the Wendys—with Darla following close behind—tromped into the kitchen, a cheerless, windowless room they had obviously tried to make homey. There were little stick dollies stuck in every possible niche and hand-painted birch bark signs on the wall.

SMILE, one sign said, YOU ARE ON CANDIED CAMERA. And another: WENDYS ARE WONDERFUL. A third, in very childish script, read: WENDYS ARE WINERS. Darla wondered idly if that was meant to be WINNERS or WHINERS, but she decided not to ask.

Depressing as the kitchen was, it was redolent with bakery smells that seemed to dissipate the effect of a prison. Darla sighed, remembering her own kitchen at home, with the windows overlooking her mother's herb garden and the rockery where four kinds of heather flowered till the first snows of winter.

The girls all sat down—on the floor, on the table, in little bumpy, woody niches. There were only two chairs in the kitchen, a tatty overstuffed chair whose gold brocaded covering had seen much better days, and a rocker. The rocker was taken by the oldest Wendy; the other chair remained empty.

At last, seeing that no one else was going to claim the stuffed chair, Darla sat down on it, and a collective gasp went up from the girls.

" 'At's Peter's chair," the littlest one finally volunteered.

"Well, Peter's not here to sit in it," Darla said. But she did not relax back against the cushion, just in case he should suddenly appear.

"I'm hungry, Wendy," said one of the girls, who had two gold braids down to her waist. "Isn't there anything left to eat?" She addressed the girl in the rocker.

"You are always hungry, Madja," Wendy said. But she smiled, and it was a smile of such sweetness, Darla was immediately reminded of her mom, in the days before the divorce and her dad's new wife.

"So you do have names, and not just Wendy," Darla said.

They looked at her as if she were stupid.

"Of course we have names," said the girl in the rocker. "I'm the only one truly named Wendy. But I've been here from the first. So that's what Peter calls us all. That's Madja," she said, pointing to the girl with the braids. "And that's Lizzy." The youngest girl. "And that's Martha, Pansy, Nina, Nancy, Heidi, Betsy, Maddy, JoAnne, Shula, Annie, Corrie, Barbara..." She went around the circle of girls.

Darla interrupted. "Then why doesn't Peter—"

"Because he can't be bothered remembering," said Wendy. "And we can't be bothered reminding him."

"And it's all right," said Madja. "Really. He has so much else to worry about. Like—"

"Him!" They all breathed the word together quietly, as if saying it aloud would summon the horror to them.

"Him? You mean Hook, don't you?" asked Darla. "Captain Hook."

The look they gave her was compounded of anger and alarm. Little Lizzy put her hands over her mouth as if she had said the name herself.

"Well, isn't it?"

"You are an extremely stupid girl," said Wendy. "As well as a dangerous one." Then she smiled again—that luminous smile—at all the other girls, excluding Darla, as if Wendy had not just said something that was both rude and horrible. "Now, darlings, how many of you are as hungry as Madja?"

One by one, the hands went up, Lizzy's first. Only

Darla kept her hand down and her eyes down as well.

"Not hungry in the slightest?" Wendy asked, and everyone went silent.

Darla felt forced to look up and saw that Wendy's eyes were staring at her, glittering strangely in the candlelight.

It was too much. Darla shivered and then, all of a sudden, she wanted to get back at Wendy, who seemed as much of a bully as Peter, only in a softer, sneakier way. *But how to do it?* And then she recalled how her mom said that telling a story in a very quiet voice always made a jury lean forward to concentrate that much more. *Maybe,* Darla thought, *I could try that.*

"I remember..." Darla began quietly. "...I remember a story my mom read to me about a Greek girl who was stolen away by the king of the underworld. He tricked her into eating six seeds and so she had to remain in the underworld six months of every year because of them."

The girls had all gone quiet and were clearly listening. *It works!* Darla thought.

"Don't be daft," Wendy said, her voice loud with authority.

"But Wendy, I remember that story, too," said the whey-faced girl, Nancy, in a kind of whisper, as if by speaking quietly she could later deny having said anything at all.

"And I," put in Madja, in a similarly whispery voice.

"And the fairies," said Lizzy. She was much too

young to worry about loud or soft, so she spoke in
her normal tone of voice. "If you eat anything in
their hall, my mum allas said...you never get to go
home again. Not ever. I miss my mum." Quite suddenly she began to cry.

"Now see what you've done," said Wendy, standing and stamping her foot. Darla was shocked. She'd
never seen anyone over four years old do such a
thing. "They'll all be blubbing now, remembering
their folks, even the ones who'd been badly beaten
at home or worse. And not a sticky bun left to com-
fort them with. You—girl—ought to be ashamed!"

"Well, it isn't my fault!" said Darla, loudly, but
she stood, too. The thought of Wendy towering over
her just now made her feel edgy and even a bit afraid.
"And my name isn't girl. It's Darla!"

They glared at one another.

Just then there was a brilliant whistle. A flash of
light circled the kitchen like a demented firefly.

"It's Tink!" Lizzy cried, clapping her hands together. "Oh! Oh! It's the signal. 'Larm! 'Larm!"

"Come on, you lot," Wendy cried. "Places, all."
She turned her back to Darla, grabbed up a soup ladle,
and ran out of the room.

Each of the girls picked up one of the kitchen
implements and followed. Not to be left behind,
Darla pounced on the only thing left, a pair of silver
sugar tongs, and pounded out after them.

They didn't go far, just to the main room again.
There they stood silent guard over the bolt-holes.

After a while—not quite fifteen minutes, Darla guessed—Tink fluttered in with a more melodic *all clear* and the boys slowly slid back down into the room.

Peter was the last to arrive.

"Oh, Peter, we were so worried," Wendy said.

The other girls crowded around. "We were scared silly," Madja added.

"Weepers!" cried Nancy.

"Knees all knocking," added JoAnne.

"Oh, this is really *too* stupid for words!" Darla said. "All we did was stand around with kitchen tools. Was I supposed to brain a pirate with these?" She held out the sugar tongs as she spoke.

The hush that followed her outcry was enormous. Without another word, Peter disappeared back into the dark. One by one, the Lost Boys followed him. Tink was the last to go, flickering out like a candle in the wind.

"Now," said Madja with a pout, "we won't even get to hear about the fight. And it's the very best part of being a Wendy."

Darla stared at the girls for a long moment. "What you all need," she said grimly, "is a backbone transplant." And when no one responded, she added, "It's clear the Wendys need to go out on strike." Being the daughter of a labor lawyer had its advantages. She knew all about strikes.

"What the Wendys *need*," Wendy responded sternly, "is to give the cupboards a good shaking-out." She patted her hair down and looked daggers at Darla. "But first, cups of tea all 'round." Turning on her heel, she started back toward the kitchen. Only four girls remained behind.

Little Lizzy crept over to Darla's side. "What's a strike?" she asked.

"Work stoppage," Darla said. "Signs and lines."

Nancy, Martha, and JoAnne, who had also stayed to listen, looked equally puzzled.

"Signs?" Nancy said.

"Lines?" Joanne said.

"*Hello*..." Darla couldn't help the exasperation in her voice. "What year do you all live in? I mean, haven't you ever heard of strikes? Watched CNN? Endured social studies?"

"Nineteen fourteen," said Martha.

"Nineteen thirty-three," said Nancy.

"Nineteen seventy-two," said Joanne.

"Do you mean to say that none of you are..." Darla couldn't think of what to call it, so added lamely, "new?"

Lizzy slipped her hand into Darla's. "You are the onliest new Wendy we've had in years."

"Oh," Darla said. "I guess that explains it." But she wasn't sure.

"Explains what?" they asked. Before Darla could answer, Wendy called from the kitchen doorway, "Are you lot coming? Tea's on." She did not sound as if she were including Darla in the invitation.

Martha scurried to Wendy's side, but Nancy and

JoAnne hesitated a moment before joining her. That left only Lizzy with Darla.

"Can I help?" Lizzy asked. "For the signs. And the 'ines? I be a good worker. Even Wendy says so."

"You're my only..." Darla said, smiling down at her and giving her little hand a squeeze. "My onliest worker. Still, as my mom always says, Start with one, you're halfway done."

Lizzy repeated the rhyme. "Start with one, you're halfway done. Start with one..."

"Just remember it. No need to say it aloud," Darla said.

Lizzy looked up at her, eyes like sky blue marbles. "But I 'ike the way that poem sounds."

"Then 'ike it quietly. We have a long way to go yet before we're ready for any chants." Darla went into the kitchen hand-in-hand with Lizzy, who skipped beside her, mouthing the words silently.

Fourteen Wendys stared at them. Not a one was smiling. Each had a teacup—unmatched, chipped, or cracked—in her hand.

"A long way to go where?" Wendy asked in a chilly voice.

"A long way before you can be free of this yoke of oppression," said Darla. *Yoke of oppression* was a favorite expression of her mother's.

"We are not yoked," Wendy said slowly. "And we are not oppressed."

"What's o-ppressed?" asked Lizzy.

"Made to do what you don't want to do," explained Darla, but she never took her eyes off of Wendy. "Treated harshly. Ruled unjustly. Governed with cruelty." Those were the three definitions she'd had to memorize for her last social studies exam. She never thought she'd ever actually get to use them in the real world. If, she thought suddenly, *this world is real.*

"No one treats us harshly or rules us unjustly. And the only cruel ones in Neverland are the pirates," Wendy explained carefully, as if talking to someone feebleminded or slow.

None of the other Wendys said a word. Most of them stared into their cups, *a little*—Darla thought— *like the way I always stare down at my shoes when Mom or Dad wants to talk about something that hurts.*

Lizzy pulled her hand from Darla's. "I think it harsh that we always have to clean up after the boys." Her voice was tiny but still it carried.

"And unjust," someone put in.

"Who said that?" Wendy demanded, staring around the table. "Who *dares* to say that Peter is unjust?"

Darla pursed her lips, wondering how her mom would answer such a question. She was about to lean forward to say something when JoAnne stood in a rush.

"I said it. And it *is* unjust. I came to Neverland to get away from that sort of thing. Well...and to get

away from my stepfather, too," she said. "I mean, I
don't mind cleaning up my own mess. And even
someone else's, occasionally. But..." She sat down
as quickly as she had stood, looking accusingly into
her cup, as if the cup had spoken and not she.

"Well!" Wendy said, sounding so much like
Darla's home ec teacher that Darla had to laugh out
loud.

As if the laugh freed them, the girls suddenly
stood up one after another, voicing complaints. And
as each one rose, little Lizzy clapped her hands and
skipped around the table, chanting, "Start with one,
you're halfway done! Start with one, you're halfway
done!"

Darla didn't say a word more. She didn't have to.
She just listened as the first trickle of angry voices
became a stream and the stream turned into a flood.
The girls spoke of the boys' mess and being under-
appreciated and wanting a larger share of the food.
They spoke about needing to go outside every once
in a while. They spoke of longing for new stockings
and a bathing room all to themselves, not one shared
with the boys, who left rings around the tub and
dirty underwear everywhere. They spoke of the long
hours and the lack of fresh air, and Barbara said they
really could use every other Saturday off, at least. It
seemed once they started complaining they couldn't
stop.

Darla's mom would have understood what had

just happened, but Darla was clearly as stunned as Wendy by the rush of demands. They stared at one another, almost like comrades.

The other girls kept on for long minutes, each one stumbling over the next to be heard, until the room positively rocked with complaints. And then, as suddenly as they had begun, they stopped. Red faced, they all sat down again, except for Lizzy, who still capered around the room, but now did it wordlessly.

Into the sudden silence, Wendy rose. "How *could* you..." she began. She leaned over the table, clutching the top, her entire body trembling. "After all Peter has done for you, taking you in when no one else wanted you, when you had been tossed aside by the world, when you'd been crushed and corrupted and canceled. How *could* you?"

Lizzy stopped skipping in front of Darla. "Is it time for signs and 'ines now?" she asked, her marble-blue eyes wide.

Darla couldn't help it. She laughed again. Then she held out her arms to Lizzy, who cuddled right in. "Time indeed," Darla said. She looked up at Wendy. "Like it or not, Miss Management, the Lost Girls are going out on strike."

Wendy sat in her rocker, arms folded, a scowl on her face. She looked like a four-year-old having a temper tantrum. But of course it was something worse than that.

The girls ignored her. They threw themselves into making signs with a kind of manic energy and in about an hour they had a whole range of them, using the backs of their old signs, pages torn from cookbooks, and flattened flour bags.

WENDYS WON'T WORK, one read. EQUAL PLAY FOR EQUAL WORK, went another. MY NAME'S NOT WENDY! said a third, and FRESH AIR IS ONLY FAIR a fourth. Lizzy's sign was decorated with stick figures carrying what Darla took to be swords, or maybe wands. Lizzy had spelled out—or rather misspelled out—what became the girls' marching words: WE AIN'T LOST, WE'RE JUST MIZ-PLAYST.

It turned out that JoAnne was musical. She made up lyrics to the tune of "Yankee Doodle Dandy" and taught them to the others:

> We ain't lost, we're just misplaced,
> The outside foe we've never faced.
> Give us a chance to fight and win
> And we'll be sure to keep Neverland neat as a pin.

The girls argued for a while over that last line, which Betsy said had too many syllables and the wrong sentiment, until Magda suggested, rather timidly, that if they actually wanted a chance to fight the pirates, maybe the boys should take a turn at cleaning the house. "Fair's fair," she added.

That got a cheer. "Fair's fair," they told one

another, and Patsy scrawled that sentiment on yet another sign.

The cheer caused Wendy to get up grumpily from her chair and leave the kitchen in a snit. She must have called for the boys then, because no sooner had the girls decided on an amended line (which still had too many syllables but felt right otherwise)—

And you can keep Neverland neat as a pin!

—than the boys could be heard coming back noisily into the dining room. They shouted and whistled and banged their fists on the table, calling out for the girls and for food. Tink's high-pitched cry overrode the noise, piercing the air. The girls managed to ignore it all until Peter suddenly appeared in the kitchen doorway.

"What's this I hear?" he said, smiling slightly to show he was more amused than angry. Somehow that only made his face seem both sinister and untrustworthy.

But his appearance in the doorway was electrifying. For a moment not one of the girls could speak. It was as if they had all taken a collective breath and were waiting to see which of them had the courage to breathe out first.

Then Lizzy held up her sign. "We're going on strike," she said brightly.

"And what, little Wendy, is that?" Peter asked,

leaning forward and speaking in the kind of voice grown-ups use with children. He pointed at her sign. "Is it..." he said slyly, "like a thimble?"

"Silly Peter," said Lizzy, "it's signs and 'ines."

"I see the signs, all right," said Peter. "But what do they mean? WENDYS WON'T WORK. Why, Neverland counts on Wendys working. And I count on it, too. You Wendys are the most important part of what we have made here."

"Oh," said Lizzy, turning to Darla, her face shining with pleasure. "*We're* the mostest important..."

Darla sighed heavily. "If you are so important, Lizzy, why can't he remember your name? If you're so important, why do you have all the work and none of the fun?"

"Right!" cried JoAnne suddenly, and immediately burst into her song. It was picked up at once by the other girls. Lizzy, caught up in the music, began to march in time all around the table with her sign. The others, still singing, fell in line behind her. They marched once around the kitchen and then right out into the dining room. Darla was at the rear.

At first the Lost Boys were stunned at the sight of the girls and their signs. Then they, too, got caught up in the song and began to pound their hands on the table in rhythm.

Tink flew around and around Wendy's head, flickering on and off and on angrily, looking for all the world like an electric hair-cutting machine. Peter glared at them all until he suddenly seemed to come to some conclusion. Then he leaped onto the dining room table, threw back his head, and crowed loudly.

At that everyone went dead silent. Even Tink.

Peter let the silence prolong itself until it was almost painful. At last he turned and addressed Darla and, through her, all the girls. "What is it you want?" he asked. "What is it you truly want? Because you'd better be careful what you ask for. In Neverland wishes are granted in very strange ways."

"It's not," Darla said carefully, "what I want. It's what *they* want."

In a tight voice, Wendy cried out, "They never wanted for anything until *she* came, Peter. They never needed or asked..."

"What we want..." JoAnne interrupted, "is to be equals."

Peter wheeled about on the table and stared down at JoAnne and she, poor thing, turned gray under his gaze. "No one is asking you," he said pointedly.

"We want to be equals!" Lizzy shouted. "To the boys. To Peter!"

The dam burst again, and the girls began shouting and singing and crying and laughing all together. "Equal...equal...equal..."

Even the boys took it up.

Tink flickered frantically, then took off up one of the bolt-holes, emerging almost immediately down another, her piercing alarm signal so loud that everyone stopped chanting, except for Lizzy, whose little voice only trailed off after a bit.

"So," said Peter, "you want equal share in the fighting? Then here's your chance."

Tink's light was sputtering with excitement and she whistled nonstop.

"Tink says Hook's entire crew is out there, waiting. And, boy! are they angry. You want to fight them? Then go ahead." He crossed his arms over his chest and turned his face away from the girls. "I won't stop you."

No longer gray but now pink with excitement, JoAnne grabbed up a knife from the nearest Lost Boy. "I'm not afraid!" she said. She headed up one of the bolt-holes.

Weaponless, Barbara, Pansy, and Betsy followed right after.

"But that's not what I meant them to do," Darla said. "I mean, weren't we supposed to work out some sort of compromise?"

Peter turned back slowly and looked at Darla, his face stern and unforgiving. "I'm Peter Pan. I don't have to compromise in Neverland." Wendy reached up to help him off the tabletop.

The other girls had already scattered up the holes, and only Lizzy was left. And Darla.

"Are you coming to the fight?" Lizzy asked Darla, holding out her hand.

Darla gulped and nodded. They walked to the

bolt-hole hand-in-hand. Darla wasn't sure what to expect, but they began rising up as if in some sort of air elevator. Behind them one of the boys was whining to Peter, "But what are we going to do without them?"

The last thing Darla heard Peter say was, "Don't worry. There are always more Wendys where they came from."

The air outside was crisp and autumny and smelled of apples. There was a full moon, orange and huge. *Harvest moon*, Darla thought, which was odd since it had been spring in her bedroom.

Ahead she saw the other girls. *And* the pirates. Or at least she saw their silhouettes. It obviously hadn't been much of a fight. The smallest of the girls—Martha, Nina, and Heidi—were already captured and riding atop their captors' shoulders. The others, with the exception of JoAnne, were being carried off fireman-style. JoAnne still had her knife and she was standing off one of the largest of the men; she got in one good swipe before being disarmed, and lifted up.

Darla was just digesting this when Lizzy was pulled from her.

"Up you go, little darlin'," came a deep voice.

Lizzy screamed. "Wendy! Wendy!"

Darla had no time to answer her before she, too, was gathered up in enormous arms and carted off.

In less time than it takes to tell of it, they were

through the woods and over a shingle, dumped into boats, and rowed out to the pirate ship. There they were hauled up by ropes and—except for Betsy, who struggled so hard she landed in the water and had to be fished out, wrung out, and then hauled up again—it was a silent and well-practiced operation.

The girls stood in a huddle on the well-lit deck and awaited their fate. Darla was glad no one said anything. She felt awful. She hadn't meant them to come to this. Peter had been right. Wishes in Neverland were dangerous.

"Here come the captains," said one of the pirates. It was the first thing anyone had said since the capture.

He must mean captain, singular, thought Darla. But when she heard footsteps nearing them and dared to look up, there were, indeed, two figures coming forward. One was an old man about her grandfather's age, his white hair in two braids, a three-cornered hat on his head. She looked for the infamous hook but he had two regular hands, though the right one was clutching a pen.

The other captain was…a woman.

"Welcome to Hook's ship," the woman said. "I'm Mrs. Hook. Also known as Mother Jane. Also known as Pirate Lil. Also called The Pirate Queen. We've been hoping we could get you away from Peter for a very long time." She shook hands with each of the girls and gave Lizzy a hug.

"I need to get to the doctor, ma'am," said one

of the pirates. "That little girl..." he pointed to JoAnne "...gave me quite a slice."

JoAnne blanched and shrank back into herself.

But Captain Hook only laughed. It was a hearty laugh, full of good humor. "Good for her. You're getting careless in your old age, Smee," he said. "Stitches will remind you to stay alert. Peter would have got your throat, and even here on the boat that could take a long while to heal."

"Now," said Mrs. Hook, "it's time for a good meal. Pizza, I think. With plenty of veggies on top. Peppers, mushrooms, carrots, onions. But no anchovies. I have never understood why anyone wants a hairy fish on top of pizza."

"What's pizza?" asked Lizzy.

"Ah...something you will love, my dear," answered Mrs. Hook. "Things never do change in Peter's Neverland, but up here on Hook's ship we move with the times."

"Who will do the dishes after?" asked Betsy cautiously.

The crew rustled behind them.

"I'm on dishes this week," said one, a burly, ugly man with a black eyepatch.

"And I," said another. She was as big as the ugly man, but attractive in a rough sort of way.

"There's a duty roster on the wall by the galley," explained Mrs. Hook. "That's ship talk for the kitchen. You'll get used to it. We all take turns. A pirate ship is a very democratic place."

"What's demo-rat-ic?" asked Lizzy.

They all laughed. "You will have a long time to learn," said Mrs. Hook. "Time moves more swiftly here than in the stuffy confines of a Neverland tree. But not so swiftly as out in the world. Now let's have that pizza, a hot bath, and a bedtime story, and then tomorrow we'll try and answer your questions."

The girls cheered, JoAnne loudest of them all.

"I am hungry," Lizzy added, as if that were all the answer Mrs. Hook needed.

"But I'm not," Darla said. "And I don't want to stay here. Not in Neverland or on Hook's ship. I want to go home."

Captain Hook came over and put his good hand under her chin. Gently he lifted her face into the light. "Father beat you?" he asked.

"Never," Darla said.

"Mother desert you?" he asked.

"Fat chance," said Darla.

"Starving? Miserable? Alone?"

"No. And no. And no."

Hook turned to his wife and shrugged. She shrugged back, then asked, "Ever think that the world was unfair, child?"

"Who hasn't?" asked Darla, and Mrs. Hook smiled.

"Thinking it and meaning it are two very different things," Mrs. Hook said at last. "I expect you must have been awfully convincing to have landed at Peter's door. Never mind, have pizza with us, and

then you can go. I want to hear the latest from outside, anyway. You never know what we might find
useful. Pizza was the last really useful thing we
learned from one of the girls we snagged before
Peter found her. And that—I can tell you—has been
a major success."

"Can't I go home with Darla?" Lizzy asked.

Mrs. Hook knelt down till she and Lizzy were
face-to-face. "I am afraid that would make for an
awful lot of awkward questions," she said.

Lizzy's blue eyes filled up with tears.

"My mom is a lawyer," Darla put in quickly.
"Awkward questions are her specialty."

The pizza was great, with a crust that was thin
and delicious. And when Darla awoke to the ticking
of the grandfather clock in the hall and the sound of
the maple branch scritch-scratching against the clapboard siding, the taste of the pizza was still in her
mouth. She felt a lump at her feet, raised up, and saw
Lizzy fast asleep under the covers at the foot of the
bed.

"I sure hope Mom is as good as I think she is,"
Darla whispered. Because there was no going back on
this one—fair, unfair, or anywhere in between.

Running in Place:
Some Thoughts Long After

In *Through the Looking-Glass* the Red Queen tells Alice that in her country it takes all the running one can do to stay in the same place. To get somewhere else, she says, "you must run at least twice as fast as that."

So it is with authors. Sometimes we don't even know what ground we have actually covered until we go back and look it over from a very great height. Only then do we notice how we have been going over a personal landscape. Only then can we see all the signposts and placards from our real lives.

Here is what I discovered when I reread these stories in preparation for putting them in this collection:

Tough Alice

I began the story as part of a class I was teaching in fantasy. I asked my students to write a variation on the Alice story, and as they worked, I tried the assignment, too. The pig image was as far as I got before our twenty minutes were up.

At the time I didn't know why I had used the pig and the reference to Pig Latin, but later I remembered. I had been a great Pig Latin devotee as a kid; even more I had liked to speak Double Dutch, which is another of those created languages. A junior high school friend and I conversed daily in that tongue, to the annoyance of everyone in both our families. In the fifties a major magazine did an article about me and my use of the invented language, along with a "cute" photograph. I found that article a couple of years ago. So that explains one line in this story.

But all stories are made up of an outside influence and an inside influence—heart and head working together. The outside influences were of course my love for the original books about Wonderland and the Looking-Glass world and my junior high Double Dutch, as well as the fact that someone I knew wanted me to write a story to go into an anthology called *Tough Girls*. I sent her "Tough Alice," then pulled it back for this collection and sent her another, which she turned down.

But there was more to it than that. The Alice in my telling is very much the child I was: timid and courageous in equal measure, looking for adventure and fearing it, too. My Alice is a child thrust into heroism kicking and screaming.

Just as the original Alice is completely a girl of

her time—that is, Carroll's references are from nineteenth-century Britain—so my Alice is a child of today. Phrases like "Haste is a terrible thing to waste," which is a twist on the education slogan "A mind is a terrible thing to waste" is a modernism that Lewis Carroll, the author of the Alice books, would never have known to use, though he loved to play with words. I am sure the careful reader can find many more.

Mama Gone

I wrote this for a volume of vampire stories I was editing, and it has ended up one of my personal favorites. My husband comes from Appalachia, from the small mountain town of Webster Springs in West Virginia. We had our honeymoon there and I am very fond of the countryside and the folksongs. But for all that there is a great beauty in those mountains, there is a shadow side, too. The coal mines have sucked the life's blood from the people; poverty has placed its dark wings over their souls.

I used to sing "All the Pretty Little Horses" to my own children at night. I am sure that the strength of the dead mother in my story—and her deep, abiding love for her own children that finally helps her master the monster she has become—is a combination of my own feelings for my children and those for my dear, departed mother, who passed away nearly thirty years ago, to my lasting sorrow

Harlyn's Fairy

I am not sure that my agent, Marilyn Marlow, knows that Aunt Marilyn is named after her. They share that same no-nonsense approach to life, though my agent is a much softer person (underneath).

I visualized the garden in our Scottish house, Wayside, as Aunt Marilyn's garden.

Harlyn, like my Alice, is also the child I used to be—imaginative, a bit secretive, a great reader of fantasy literature (though I didn't get to read *The Hobbit* until I was an adult). But I had a depressingly ordinary family, no major quirks or jerks. Except for a couple of cousins and an uncle I could mention...

Phoenix Farm

We named our house in Massachusetts Phoenix Farm when we moved in. Actually I wanted to name it Fe-Fi-Fo-Farm but my husband, who normally has a giant sense of humor, absolutely refused.

Sea Dragon of Fife

Our summer house is in Scotland, in St. Andrews, which is in the Kingdom of Fife. That is what it is actually called—Kingdom—though it is really a state or a county.

I had written a comic book, *The Great Selchie*, that I set in Anstruther (or Anster, as the locals call it), one of the little fishing villages on the Fife coast near our house. My best friend in Scotland lives there. I did a lot of research into nineteenth-century Scottish folk-life in the Scottish Fisheries Museum, and I only got to use a small bit of it for the comic. Never the kind of author to waste anything, especially research, I decided to write a short story set in the same place and time. Bruce Coville was looking for monster stories and so it went to him. He bought it and called it "a thrilling sea yarn." But anything "thrilling" in the story I credit to the seas around Scotland, which summer or winter are both gorgeous and—on occasion—treacherous as well.

Wilding

I was born and brought up in New York City and lived most of the first thirteen years of my life in an apartment house on the corner of Central Park West and Ninety-Seventh Street, right next to the First Church of Christian Science. That is the exact setting of Wild Wood Central. My brother and best friend, Diane, and I used to play in the park where Zena and her pals go, though we played baseball, cowboys and Indians, and Knights of the Round Table, not Wilding.

The reference to Max and the Wild Things being "an old story" is, of course, a nod to Maurice Sendak's picture book *Where the Wild Things Are*. It is a story in which a child's wildness is tamed by his imagination, which is a healthy outlet for that kind of thing. However, the actual term *Wilding* was one that arose in the late 1980s, when gangs of teenagers and young adults ran savagely through Central Park, mugging, raping, and beating up people whose only sin was to be in the wrong place at the wrong time. I'd like to think that we can tame our wildness or at least channel it into more acceptable behaviors, and my story is about that possibility.

The Baby-Sitter

The house in this story is actually my Massachusetts house, which has a long, dark, windowless hall upstairs. My middle son used to be so frightened of that hall and the monsters he believed were hiding in the cupboards that he actually invented an entire set of rituals. They included turning around and touching parts of the walls to keep him safe. Nowadays he is a rock-and-roll musician, which involves another group of rituals. I am not sure they keep him very safe at all.

The incident with the cheerleading outfit comes directly out of a confrontation my daughter—who was captain of the cheerleaders when she was in high school—had with her school principal. Her friend Brenda really had been sent home from school because her skirt was too short.

I originally wrote this story just to be scary. I think a lot of childhood fears crept into it. And the fears I have now, when I am occasionally alone in my big house.

Bolundeers

The setting is my son Adam's old room, which looks out over the corner of the garden where there used to be a compost heap. The first seven years we lived in this house in Hatfield, Massachusetts, I had a large vegetable garden. My children loved to graze in it, eating fresh peas right out of the pods. Now I have things I'd rather do than spend hours weeding. Like writing. And reading. And taking long walks. So I cultivate my gardening friends rather than my own plot of land, and they give me their overruns.

Since our three children are grown-up and have moved away, my husband and I have taken over Adam's room. It's a lot quieter than ours, which overlooks the street, but it is rather full of his old ghosts. I used to sit by his bed for hours, singing to him and reassuring him when he was a child. A lot of that was in the first draft of the story.

I wrote "Bolundeers" for *A Nightmare's Dozen*. The editor made me rewrite it over and over, each time asking for it to be scarier and spookier, which was difficult, given those memories.

The first time through the story, the ghost sang "All the Pretty Little Horses." And then I remembered I had used that song in "Mama Gone." So I changed it to "Dance to Your Daddy," another song I loved to sing to my own kids to get them to fall asleep.

The Bridge's Complaint

The idea of telling the story of "The Three Billy Goats Gruff" from the bridge's viewpoint came from a boy who called in to an educational TV show I was doing in Boston. "Trot, trot, trot," he said, "all day long." I broke up on camera.

It took me about five years after that call before I could figure out how to pull the entire story off. Alas, I don't remember the boy's name—but my thanks to him anyway.

Brandon and the Aliens

One of my best friends is Bruce Coville. Sometimes he gets me to do things I don't actually want to do, such as stay up too late at parties or ride the New York subway. And sometimes he influences my writing. This story has a couple of things that Bruce is famous for: urpy monsters and slime. Bruce put this story in one of his anthologies, his *Book of Aliens II*. The editor there made me take out the enema line. I whined, "But Bruce had a group fart in one of his stories!" She answered, "I knew I was going to regret letting him do that!" The enema line never made it into Bruce's anthology, but I decided to put it back in this collection.

Brandon is my son-in-law's name. I thought it might be fun to put him in a story. He wasn't a hockey player as a kid, though. He was a surfer.

Freddy is named after my favorite cousin. No one else I know is in the story. Especially not the aliens. (Though Bruce probably knows them!)

Winter's King

The wonderful science fiction–fantasy artist Dawn Wilson created a pair of stunning paintings called *Winter's King* and *Winter's Queen*. She then asked a number of fantasy authors to write stories to go with the paintings. But Dawn's proposed anthology never actually sold to any publisher. I had started my story but had not gotten beyond the first scene when the news that the project had died reached me. So I put that first scene away in the "Large File."

Several years passed. And then I heard from another editor that he was doing a Tolkien memorial anthology and wanted a story from me. I had no ideas. (Trust me, this happens more often than you would think.) So I got out the Large File and looked in it to see if anything inspired me.

And there was the opening of "Winter's King." Just the first page. I wasn't sure exactly where it was going but it seemed to want me to try.

I tried.

Sometimes the magic works.

Lost Girls

The opening scene of this story, with Darla in her bed complaining about the girls in Neverland, came to me one evening. I have no idea why. I think Darla reminded me of my daughter at that age who had always whined, "It's not fair!" About everything.

But nothing more happened, so the story starter got put in the ubiquitous Large File.

When Marilyn Singer asked me to contribute to her anthology *Tough Girls*, I hauled the paragraphs out of the Large File and tried to make it go somewhere. It refused.

Sometimes the magic doesn't work.

I carried the manuscript back and forth with me across the Atlantic, hoping that a story would emerge somewhere, sometime. I noodled away at it, meaning I would add a line, take out a phrase, change a word, break one sentence into two. But nothing more happened. The plot steadfastly refused to gel. So I sent a different story (see the "Tough Alice" note) to the editor of *Tough Girls*.

And then one day I hauled the story out and wrote about half of it. I have no idea why.

Sometimes the magic works.

Then I got stuck again. I thought the problem was that it might rather be the start of a novel. Clearly it was already much longer than most of my usual stories.

And then again sometimes the magic creaks to a halt.

As I was now hard at work on this collection, I sent the finished half of "Lost Girls" on to my editor.

"Is this a novel?" I asked.

"It's a short story," he answered.

Immediately I got back to work on it. I named the Lost Girls after friends and family: my daughter, Heidi, my daughter-in-law, Betsy, my youngest son's girlfriend, JoAnne, and a bunch of the writers in my Tuesday group. The rest of the story just fell into place.

Sometimes the magic does work.

Really!

Let your imagination fly with the best in fantasy

MAGIC
CARPET

BOOKS

DIANE DUANE's thrilling wizardry series

So You Want to Be a Wizard (0-15-201239-7) $6.50
Fleeing a bully, Nita discovers a manual on wizardry in her library. But magic
doesn't solve her problems—in fact, they've only just begun!

Deep Wizardry (0-15-201240-0) $6.00
The novice wizards join a group of dolphins, whales, and one giant shark in an
ancient magical ritual—a ritual that must end with a bloody sacrifice.

High Wizardry (0-15-201241-9) $6.00
Nita and Kit face their most terrifying challenge yet: Nita's bratty little sister,
Dairine—the newest wizard in the neighborhood!

A Wizard Abroad (0-15-201207-9) $6.00
Nita's Irish vacation from magic turns out to be the opposite! Ireland is even more
steeped in wizardly dangers than the States. So much for a vacation abroad....

The Forgotten Beasts of Eld (0-15-200869-1) $6.00
BY PATRICIA A. McKILLIP
Sybel's only family is the group of animals that live on Eld Mountain. She cares
nothing for humans until she is given a child to raise, changing her life utterly.

EDITH PATTOU's epic Songs of Eirren

Hero's Song (0-15-201636-8) $6.00
The trail of his sister's kidnappers leads Collun to a giant white wurme whose
slime is acid to the touch, a wurme that Collun must kill if he is to rescue his
sister and save his world.

Fire Arrow (0-15-202264-3) $6.00
Archer Breo-Saight ("Fire Arrow") is hunting her father's murderers. Her
vendetta leads to a distant land where she finds the family she never had...and a
sorcerer's evil magic. To save the people she's grown to love, she must follow
her revenge to its bitter end.